Lester del Rey

The Sky Is Falling
(SF Classic)

OK Publishing 2021

Lester del Rey
The Sky Is Falling

(SF Classic)

Published by
MUSAICUM
Books

- Advanced Digital Solutions & High-Quality book Formatting -

musaicumbooks@okpublishing.info

2021 OK Publishing

ISBN 978-80-272-7426-0

Contents

Dave stared around the office. He went to the window and stared upwards at the crazy patchwork of the sky. For all he knew, in such a sky there might be cracks. In fact, as he looked, he could make out a rift, and beyond that a ...hole ...a small patch where there was no color, and yet the sky there was not black. There were no stars there, though points of light were clustered around the edges, apparently retreating.

I

"Dave Hanson! By the power of the true name be summoned cells and humors, ka and id, self and — "

Dave Hanson! The name came swimming through utter blackness, sucking at him, pulling him together out of nothingness. Then, abruptly, he was aware of being alive, and surprised. He sucked in on the air around him, and the breath burned in his lungs. He was one of the dead — there should be no quickening of breath within him!

He caught a grip on himself, fighting the fantasies of his mind, and took another breath of air. This time it burned less, and he could force an awareness of the smells around him. But there was none of the pungent odor of the hospital he had expected. Instead, his nostrils were scorched with a noxious odor of sulfur, burned hair and cloying incense.

He gagged on it. His diaphragm tautened with the sharp pain of long-unused muscles, and he sneezed.

"A good sign," a man's voice said. "The followers have accepted and are leaving. Only a true being can sneeze. But unless the salamander works, his chances are only slight."

There was a mutter of agreement from others, before an older voice broke in. "It takes a deeper fire than most salamanders can stir, Ser Perth. We might aid it with high-frequency radiation, but I distrust the effects on the prepsyche. If we tried a tamed succubus — "

"The things are untrustworthy," the first voice an swered. "And with the sky falling, we dare not trust one."

The words blurred off in a fog of semiconsciousness and half-thoughts. The sky was falling? Who killed Foxy Loxy? I, said the spider, who sat down insider, I went boomp in the night and the bull jumped over the moon....

"Bull," he croaked. "The bull sleeper!"

"Delirious," the first voice muttered.

"I mean — bull pusher!" That was wrong, too, and he tried again, forcing his reluctant tongue around the syllables. "Bull *dosser!*"

Damn it, couldn't he even pronounce simple Engaliss?

The language wasn't English, however. Nor was it Canadian French, the only other speech he could make any sense of. Yet he understood it — had even spoken it, he realized. There was nothing wrong with his command of whatever language it was, but there seemed to be no word for bulldozer. He struggled to get his eyes open.

The room seemed normal enough, in spite of the odd smells. He lay on a high bed, sur-rounded by prim white walls, and there was even a chart of some kind at the bottom of the bedframe. He focused his eyes slowly on what must be the doctors and nurses there, and their faces looked back with the proper professional worry. But the varicolored gowns they wore in place of proper clothing were covered with odd designs, stars, crescents and things that might have been symbols for astronomy or chemistry.

He tried to reach for his glasses to adjust them. There were no glasses! That hit him harder than any other discovery. He must be delirious and imagining the room. Dave Hanson was so nearsighted that he couldn't have seen the men, much less the clothing, without corrective lenses.

The middle-aged man with the small mustache bent over the chart near his feet. "Hmm," the man said in the voice of the first speaker. "Mars trines Neptune. And with Scorpio so altered ... hmm. Better add two cc. of cortisone to the transfusion."

Hanson tried to sit up, but his arms refused to bear his weight. He opened his mouth. A slim hand came to his lips, and he looked up into soothing blue eyes. The nurse's face was framed in copper-red hair. She had the transparent skin and classic features that occur once in a million times but which still keep the legend of redheaded enchantresses alive. "Shh," she said.

He began to struggle against her hand, but she shook her head gently. Her other hand began a series of complicated motions that had a ritualistic look about them.

"Shh," she repeated. "Rest. Relax and sleep, Dave Hanson, and remember when you were alive."

There was a sharp sound from the doctor, but it began to blur out before Hanson could understand it. He fought to remember what he'd heard the nurse say — something about when he was alive — as if he'd been dead a long time....He couldn't hold the thought. At a final rapid motion of the girl's hand his eyes closed, the smell faded from his nose and all sounds vanished. Once there was a stinging sensation, as if he were receiving the transfusion. Then he was alone in his mind with his memories — mostly of the last day when he'd still been alive. He seemed to be reliving the events, rethinking the thoughts he'd had then.

It began with the sight of his uncle's face leering at him. Uncle David Arnold Hanson looked like every man's dream of himself and every woman's dreams of manliness. But at the moment, to Dave, he looked more like a personal demon. His head was tilted back and nasty laughter was booming through the air of the little office.

"So your girl writes that your little farewell activity didn't fare so well, eh?" he chortled. "And you come crawling here to tell me you want to do the honorable thing, is that it? All right, my beloved nephew, you'll do the honorable thing! You'll stick to your contract with me."

"But — " Dave began.

"But if you don't, you'd better read it again. You don't get one cent except on completion of your year with me. That's what it says, and that's what happens." He paused, letting the fact that he meant it sink in. He was enjoying the whole business, and in no hurry to end it. "And I happen to know, Dave, that you don't even have fare to Saskatchewan left. You quit and I'll see you never get another job. I promised my sister I'd make a man of you and, by jumping Jupiter, I intend to do just that. And in my book, that doesn't mean you run back with your tail between your legs just because some silly young girl pulls that old chestnut on you. Why, when I was your age, I already had...."

Dave wasn't listening any longer. In futile anger, he'd swung out of the office and gone stumbling back toward the computer building. Then, in a further burst of anger, he swung off the trail. To hell with his work and blast his uncle! He'd go on into town, and he'd — he'd do whatever he pleased.

The worst part of it was that Uncle David could make good on his threat of seeing that Dave got no more work anywhere. David Arnold Hanson was a power to reckon with. No other man on Earth could have persuaded anyone to let him try his scheme of building a great deflection wall across northern Canada to change the weather patterns. And no other man could have accomplished the impossible task, even after twelve countries pooled their resources to give him the job. But he was doing it, and it was already beginning to work. Dave had noticed that the last winter in Chicago had definitely shown that Uncle David's predictions were coming true.

Like most of the world, Dave had regarded the big man who was his uncle with something close to worship. He'd jumped at the chance to work under Uncle David. And he'd been a fool. He'd been doing all right in Chicago. Repairing computers didn't pay a fortune, but it was a good living, and he was good at it. And there was Bertha — maybe not a movie doll, but a sort of pretty girl who was also a darned good cook. For a man of thirty who'd always been a scrawny, shy runt like the one in the "before" pictures, he'd been doing all right.

Then came the letter from his uncle, offering him triple salary as a maintenance man on the computers used for the construction job. There was nothing said about romance and beauteous Indian maids, but Dave filled that in himself. He would need the money when he and Bertha got married, too, and all that healthy outdoor living was just what the doctor would have ordered.

The Indian maids, of course, turned out to be a few fat old squaws who knew all about white men. The outdoor living developed into five months of rain, hail, sleet, blizzard, fog and constant freezing in tractors while breathing the healthy fumes of diesels. Uncle David turned out to be a construction genius, all right, but his interest in Dave seemed to lie in the fact that he was tired of being Simon Legree to strangers and wanted to take it out on one of his own family.

And the easy job turned into hell when the regular computer-man couldn't take any more and quit, leaving Dave to do everything, including making the field tests to gain the needed data.

Now Bertha was writing frantic letters, telling him how much he'd better come back and marry her immediately. And Uncle David thought it was a joke!

Dave paid no attention to where his feet were leading him, only vaguely aware that he was heading down a gully below the current construction job. He heard the tractors and bulldozers moving along the narrow cliff above him, but he was used to the sound. He heard frantic yelling from above, too, but paid no attention to it; in any Hanson construction program, somebody was always yelling about something that had to be done day before yesterday. It wasn't until he finally became aware of his own name being shouted that he looked up. Then he froze in horror.

The bulldozer was teetering at the edge of the cliff as he saw it, right above him. And the cliff was crumbling from under it, while the tread spun idiotically out of control. As Dave's eyes took in the whole situation, the cliff crumbled completely, and the dozer came lunging over the edge, plunging straight for him. His shout was drowned in the roar of the motor. He tried to force his legs to jump, but they were frozen in terror. The heavy mass came straight for him, its treads churning like great teeth reaching for him.

Then it hit, squarely on top of him. Something ripped and splattered and blacked out in an unbearable welter of agony.

Dave Hanson came awake trying to scream and thrusting at the bed with arms too weak to raise him. The dream of the past was already fading. The horror he had thought was death lay somewhere in the past.

Now he was here — wherever here was.

The obvious answer was that he was in a normal hospital, somehow still alive, being patched up. The things he seemed to remember from his other waking must be a mixture of fact and delirium. Besides, how was he to judge what was normal in extreme cases of surgery?

He managed to struggle up to a sitting position in the bed, trying to make out more of his surroundings. But the room was dark now. As his eyes adjusted, he made out a small brazier there, with a cadaverous old man in a dark robe spotted with looped crosses. On his head was something like a miter, carrying a coiled brass snake in front of it. The old man's white goatee bobbed as he mouthed something silently and made passes over the flame, which shot up prismatically. Clouds of white fire belched up.

Dave reached to adjust his glasses, and found again that he wasn't wearing them. But he'd never seen so clearly before.

At that moment, a chanting voice broke into his puzzled thoughts. It sounded like Ser Perth. Dave turned his head weakly. The motion set sick waves of nausea running through him, but he could see the doctor kneeling on the floor in some sort of pantomime. The words of the chant were meaningless.

A hand closed over Dave's eyes, and the voice of the nurse whispered in his ear. "Shh, Dave Hanson. It's the Sather Karf, so don't interrupt. There may be a conjunction."

He fell back, panting, his heart fluttering. Whatever was going on, he was in no shape to interrupt anything. But he knew that this was no delirium. He didn't have that kind of imagination.

The chant changed, after a long moment of silence. Dave's heart had picked up speed, but now it missed again, and he felt cold. He shivered. Hell or heaven weren't like this, either. It was like something out of some picture — something about Cagliostro, the ancient mystic. But he was sure the language he somehow spoke wasn't an ancient one. It had words for electron, penicillin and calculus, for he found them in his own mind.

The chant picked up again, and now the brazier flamed a dull red, showing the Sather Karf's face changing from some kind of disappointment to a businesslike steadiness. The red glow grew white in the center, and a fat, worm-like shape of flame came into being. The old man picked it up in his hand, petted it and carried it toward Dave. It flowed toward his chest.

He pulled himself back, but Ser Perth and the nurse leaped forward to hold him. The thing started to grow brighter. It shone now like a tiny bit of white-hot metal; but the older man touched it, and it snuggled down into Dave's chest, dimming its glow and somehow purring. Warmth seemed to flow from it into Dave. The two men watched for a moment, then picked up their apparatus and turned to go. The Sather Karf lifted the fire from the brazier in his bare hand, moved it into the air and said a soft word. It vanished, and the two men were also gone.

"Magic!" Dave said. He'd seen such illusions created on the stage, but there was something different here. And there was no fakery about the warmth from the thing over his chest. Abruptly he remembered that he'd come across something like it, called a salamander, in fiction once; the thing was supposed to be a spirit of fire, and dangerously destructive.

The girl nodded in the soft glow coming from Dave's chest. "Naturally," she told him. "How else does one produce and control a salamander, except by magic? Without, magic, how can we thaw a frozen soul? Or didn't your world have any sciences, Dave Hanson?"

Either the five months under his uncle had toughened him, or the sight of the bulldozer falling had knocked him beyond any strong reaction. The girl had practically told him he wasn't in his own world. He waited for some emotion, felt none, and shrugged. The action sent pain running through him, but he stood it somehow. The salamander ceased its purring, then resumed.

"Where in hell am I?" he asked. "Or when?"

She shook her head. "Hell? No, I don't think so. Some say it's Earth and some call it Terah, but nobody calls it Hell. It's — well, it's a long — time, I guess — from when you were. I don't know. In such matters, only the Satheri know. The Dual is closed even to the Seri. Anyhow, it's not your space-time, though some say it's your world."

"You mean dimensional travel?" Dave asked. He'd seen something about that on a science-fiction television program. It made even time travel seem simple. At any event, however, this wasn't a hospital in any sane and normal section of Canada during his time, on Earth.

"Something like that," she agreed doubtfully. "But go to sleep now. Shh." Her hands came up in complicated gestures. "Sleep and grow well."

"None of that hypnotism again!" he protested.

She went on making passes, but smiled on him kindly. "Don't be superstitious — hypnotism is silly. Now go to sleep. For me, Dave Hanson. I want you well and true when you awake."

Against his will, his eyes closed, and his lips refused to obey his desire to protest. Fatigue dulled his thoughts. But for a moment, he went on pondering. Somebody from the future — this could never be the past — had somehow pulled him out just ahead of the accident, apparently; or else he'd been deep frozen somehow to wait for medical knowledge beyond that of his own time. He'd heard it might be possible to do that.

It was a cockeyed future, if this were the future. Still, if scientists had to set up some, sort of a religious mumbo-jumbo....

Sickness thickened in him, until he could feel his face wet with perspiration. But with it had come a paralysis that left him unable to move or groan. He screamed inside himself.

"Poor mandrake-man," the girl said softly. "Go back to Lethe. But don't cross over. We need you sorely."

Then he passed out again.

II

Whatever they had done to patch him up hadn't been very successful, apparently. He spent most of the time in a delirium; sometimes he was dead, and there was an ultimate coldness like the universe long after the entropy death. At other times, he was wandering into fantasies that were all horrible. And at all times, even in unconsciousness, he seemed to be fighting desperately to keep from falling apart painfully within himself.

When he was awake, the girl was always beside him. He learned that her name was Nema. Usually there was also the stout figure of Ser Perth. Sometimes he saw Sather Karf or some other older man working with strange equipment, or with things that looked like familiar hypodermics and medical equipment. Once they had an iron lung around him and there was a thin wisp over his face.

He started to brush it aside, but Nema's hand restrained him. "Don't disturb the sylph," she ordered.

Another semirational period occurred during some excitement or danger that centered around him. He was still half delirious, but he could see men working frantically to build a net of something around his bed, while a wet, thick thing flopped and drooled beyond the door, apparently immune to the attacks of the hospital staff. There were shouting orders involving the undine. The salamander in Dave's chest crept deeper and seemed to bleat at each cry of the monstrous thing beyond the door.

Sather Karf sat hunched over what seemed to be a bowl of water, paying no attention to the struggle. Something that he seemed to see there held his attention. Then he screamed suddenly.

"The Sons of the Egg. It's their sending!"

He reached for a brazier beside him, caught up the fire and plunged it deep into the bowl of water, screaming something. There was the sound of an explosion from far away as he drew his hands out, unwet by the water. Abruptly the undine began a slow retreat. In Dave's chest, the salamander began purring again, and he drifted back into his coma.

He tried to ask Nema about it later when she was feeding him, but she brushed it aside.

"An orderly let out the news that you are here," she said. "But don't worry. We've sent out a doppelganger to fool the Sons, and the orderly has been sentenced to slavery under the pyramid builder for twenty lifetimes. I hate my brother! How dare he fight us with the sky falling?"

Later, the delirium seemed to pass completely, but Dave took no comfort from that. In its place came a feeling of gloom and apathy. He slept most of the time, as if not daring to use his little strength even to think.

Ser Perth stayed near him most of the time now. The man was obviously worried, but tried not to show it. "We've managed to get some testosterone from a blond homunculus," he reported. "That should put you on your feet in no time. Don't worry, young man we'll keep you vivified somehow until the Sign changes." But he didn't sound convincing.

"Everyone is chanting for you," Nema told him. "All over the world, the chants go up."

It meant nothing to him, but it sounded friendly. A whole world hoping for him to get well! He cheered up a bit at that until he found out that the chants were compulsory, and had nothing to do with goodwill.

The iron lung was back the next time he came to, and he was being tugged toward it. He noticed this time that there was no sylph, and his breathing seemed to be no worse than usual. But the sight of the two orderlies and the man in medical uniform beside the lung reassured him. Whatever their methods, he was convinced that they were doing their best for him here.

He tried to help them get him into the lung, and one of the men nodded encouragingly. But Dave was too weak to give much assistance. He glanced about for Nema, but she was out on one of her infrequent other duties. He sighed, wishing desperately that she were with him. She was a lot more proficient than the orderlies.

The man in medical robe turned toward him sharply. "Stop that!" he ordered.

Before Dave could ask what he was to stop, Nema came rushing into the room. Her face paled as she saw the three men, and she gasped, throwing up her hand in a protective gesture.

The two orderlies jumped for her, one grabbing her and the other closing his hands over her mouth. She struggled violently, but the men were too strong for her.

The man in doctor's robes shoved the iron lung aside violently and reached into his clothing. From it, he drew a strange, double-bladed knife. He swung toward Dave, raising the knife into striking position and aiming it at Dave's heart.

"The Egg breaks," he intoned hollowly. It was a cultured voice, and there was a refinement to his face that registered on Dave's mind even over the horror of the weapon. "The fools cannot hold the shell. But neither shall they delay its breaking. Dead you were, mandrake son, and dead you shall be again. But since the fault is only theirs, may no ill dreams follow you beyond Lethe!"

The knife started down, just as Nema managed to break free. She shrieked out a phrase of keening command. The salamander suddenly broke from Dave's chest, glowing brighter as it rose toward the face of the attacker. It was like a bit from the center of a star. The man jumped back, beginning a frantic ritual. He was too late. The salamander hit him, sank into him and shone through him. Then he slumped, steamed ... and was nothing but dust falling toward the carpet. The salamander turned, heading toward the others. But it was to Nema it went, rather than the two men. She was trying something desperately, but fear was thick on her face, and her hands were unsure.

Abruptly, Sather Karf was in the doorway. His hand lifted, his fingers dancing. Words hissed from his lips in a stream of sibilants too quick for Dave to catch. The salamander paused and began to shrink doubtfully. Sather Karf turned, and again his hands writhed in the air. One hand darted back and forward, as if he were throwing something. Again he made the gesture. With each throw, one of the false orderlies dropped to the floor, clutching at a neck where the skin showed marks of constriction as if a steel cord were tightening. They died slowly, their eyes bulging and faces turning blue. Now the salamander moved toward them, directed apparently by slight motions from Sather Karf. In a few moments, there was no sign of them.

The old man sighed, his face slumping into lines of fatigue and age. He caught his breath. He held out a hand to the salamander, petted it to a gentle glow and put it back over Dave's chest.

"Good work, Nema," he said wearily. "You're too weak to control the salamander, but this was done well in the emergency. I saw them in the pool, but I was almost too late. The damned fanatics. Superstition in this day and age!"

He swung to face Dave, whose vocal cords were still taut with the shock of the sight of the knife. "Don't worry, Dave Hanson. From now on, every Ser and Sather will protect you with the lower and the upper magic. The House changes tomorrow, if the sky permits, and we shall shield you until then. We didn't bring you back from the dead, piecing your scattered atoms together with your scattered revenant particle by particle, to have you killed again. Somehow, we'll incarnate you fully! You have my word for that."

"Dead?" Dave had grown numbed to his past during the long illness, but that brought it back afresh. "Then I was killed? I wasn't just frozen and brought here by some time machine?"

Sather Karf stared at him blankly. "Time machine? Impossible. Of course not. After the tractor killed you, and you were buried, what good would such fantasies be, even if they existed? No, we simply reincarnated you by pooling our magic. Though it was a hazardous and parlous thing, with the sky falling...."

He sighed and went out, while Dave went back to his delirium.

III

There was no delirium when he awoke in the morning. Instead, there was only a feeling of buoyant health. In fact, Dave Hanson had never felt that good in his life — or his former life. He reconsidered his belief that there was no delirium, wondering if the feeling were not itself a form of hallucination. But it was too genuine. He knew without question that he was well.

It shouldn't have been true. During the night, he'd partially awakened in agony to find Nema chanting and gesturing desperately beside him, and he'd been sure he was on the verge of his second death. He could remember one moment, just before midnight, when she had stopped and seemed to give up hope. Then she'd braced herself and begun some ritual as if she were afraid to try it. Beyond that, he had no memory of pain.

Nema came into the room now, touching his shoulder gently. She smiled and nodded at him. "Good morning, Sagittarian. Get out of bed."

Expecting the worst, he swung his feet over the side and sat up. After so much time in bed, even a well man should be rendered weak and shaky. But there was no dizziness, no sign of weakness. He had made a most remarkable recovery, and Nema didn't even seem surprised. He tentatively touched foot to floor and half stood, propping himself against the high bed.

"Come on," Nema said impatiently. "You're all right now. We entered your sign during the night." She turned her back on him and took something from a chest beside the bed. "Ser Perth will be here in a moment. He'll want to find you on your feet and dressed."

Hanson was beginning to feel annoyance at the suddenly cocksure and unsympathetic girl, but he stood fully erect and flexed his muscles. There wasn't even a trace of bedsoreness, though he had been flat on his back long enough to grow callouses. And as he examined himself, he could find no scars or signs of injuries from the impact of the bulldozer — if there had ever really been a bulldozer.

He grimaced at his own doubts. "Where am I, anyhow, Nema?"

The girl dumped an armload of clothing on his bed and looked at him with controlled exasperation. "Dave Hanson," she told him, "don't you know any other words? That's the millionth time you've asked me that, at least. And for the hundredth time, I'll tell you that you're here. Look around you; see for yourself. I'm tired of playing nursemaid to you." She picked up a shirt of heavy-duty khaki from the pile on the bed and handed it to him. "Get into this," she ordered. "Dress first, talk later."

She stalked out of the room.

Dave did as she had ordered, busy with his own thoughts as he discovered what he was to wear. He was still wearing something with a vague resemblance to a short hospital gown, with green pentacles and some plant symbol woven into it, and with a clasp to hold it together shaped into a silver crux ansata. He took it off and hurled it into a corner disgustedly.

He picked up the khaki shirt and put it on; then, with growing curiosity, the rest of the garments, until he came to the shoes. Khaki shirt, khaki breeches, a wide, webbed belt, a flat-brimmed hat. And the shoes — they weren't shoes, but knee-length leather boots, like a dressy version of lumberman's boots or a rougher version of riding boots. He hadn't seen even pictures of such things since the few silent movies run in some of the little art theaters. He struggled to get them on. They were an excellent fit, and comfortable enough, but he felt as if his legs were encased in hardened concrete when he was through. He looked down at himself in disgust. He was in all respects costumed as the epitome of the Hollywood dream of a heroic engineer-builder, ready to drive a canal through an isthmus or throw a dam across a raging river — the kind who'd build the dam while the river raged, instead of waiting until it was quiet, a few days later. He was about as far from the appearance of the actual blue-denim, leather-jacket engineers he had worked with as Maori in ancient battle array.

He shook his head and went looking for the bathroom, where there might be a mirror. He found a door, but it led into a closet, filled with alembics and other equipment. There was a mirror hung on the back of it, however, with a big sign over it that said "Keep Out." He threw the door wide and stared at himself. At first, in spite of the costume, he was pleased. Then the truth began to hit him, and he felt abruptly sure he was still raging with fever and delirium.

He was still staring when Nema came back into the room. She pursed her lips and shut the door quickly. But he'd already seen enough.

"Never mind where I am," he said. "Tell me, *who* am I?"

She stared at him. "You're Dave Hanson."

"The hell I am," he told her. "Oh, that's what I remember my father having me christened as. He hated long names. But take a good look at me. I've been shaving my face for years now, and I should know it. *That* face in the mirror wasn't it! There's a resemblance. But a darned faint one. Change the chin, lengthen my nose, make the eyes brown instead of blue, and it might be me. But Dave Hanson's at least five inches shorter and fifty pounds lighter, too. Maybe the face is plastic surgery after the accident — but this isn't even my body."

The girl's expression softened. "I'm sorry, Dave Hanson," she said gently. "We should have thought to warn you. You were a difficult conjuration — and even the easier ones often go wrong these days. We did our best, though it may be that the auspices were too strong on the soma. I'm sorry if you don't like the way you look. But there's nothing we can do about it now."

Hanson opened the door again, in spite of Nema's quick frown, and looked at himself. "Well," he admitted, "I guess it could be worse. In fact, I guess it was worse — once I get used to looking like this, I think I'll get to like it. But seeing it was a heck of a thing to take for a sick man."

Nema said sharply, "Are you sick?"

"Well — I guess not."

"Then why say you are? You shouldn't be; I told you we've entered the House of Sagittarius now. You can't be sick in your own sign. Don't you understand even that much elementary science?"

Hanson didn't get a chance to answer. Ser Perth was suddenly in the doorway, dressed in a different type of robe. This was short and somehow conservative — it had a sincere, executive look about it. The man seemed changed in other ways, too. But Dave wasn't concerned about that. He was growing tired of the way people suddenly appeared out of nowhere. Maybe they all wore rubber-soled shoes or practiced sneaking about; it was a silly way for grown people to act.

"Come with me, Dave Hanson," Ser Perth ordered, without wasting words. He spoke in a clipped manner now.

Dave followed, grumbling in his mind. It was even sillier than their sneaking about for them to expect him to start running around before they bothered to check the condition of a man fresh out of his death bed. In any of the hospitals he had known, there would have been hours or days of X-rays and blood tests and temperature taking before he would be released. These people simply decided a man was well and ordered him out.

To do them justice, however, he had to admit that they seemed to be right. He had never felt better. The twaddle about Sagittarius would have to be cleared up sometime, but meanwhile he was in pretty good shape. Sagittarius, as he remembered it, was supposed to be one of the signs of the Zodiac. Bertha had been something of a sucker for astrology and had found he was born under that sign before she agreed to their little good-by party. He snorted to himself. It had done her a heck of a lot of good, which was to be expected of such nonsense.

They passed down a dim corridor and Ser Perth turned in at a door. Inside there was a single-chair barber shop, with a barber who might also have come from some movie-casting office. He had the proper wavy black hair and rat-tailed comb stuck into a slightly dirty off-white jacket. He also had the half-obsequious, half-insulting manner Dave had found most people expected from their barbers. While he shaved and trimmed Dave, he made insultingly solicitous comments about Dave's skin needing a massage, suggested a tonic for thinning hair and practically insisted on a singe. Ser Perth watched with a mixture of intentness and amusement. The barber trimmed the tufts from over Dave's ears and clipped the hair in his nose, while a tray was pushed up and a slatternly blonde began giving him a manicure.

He began noticing that she carefully dumped his fingernail parings into a small jar. A few moments later, he found the barber also using a jar to collect the hair and shaving stubble. Ser Perth was also interested in that, it seemed, since his eyes followed that part of the operation. Dave frowned, and then relaxed. After all, this was a hospital barber shop, and they probably had some rigid rules about sanitation, though he hadn't seen much other evidence of such care.

The barber finally removed the cloth with a snap and bowed. "Come again, sir," he said.

Ser Perth stood up and motioned for Dave to follow. He turned to look in a mirror, and caught sight of the barber handing the bottles and jars of waste hair and nail clippings to a girl. He saw only her back, but it looked like Nema.

Something stirred in his mind then. He'd read something somewhere about hair clippings and nail parings being used for some strange purpose. And there'd been something about spittle. But they hadn't collected that. Or had they? He'd been unconscious long enough for them to have gathered any amount they wanted. It all had something to do with some kind of mumbo-jumbo, and....

Ser Perth had led him through the same door by which they'd entered — but *not* into the same hallway. Dave's mind dropped the other thoughts as he tried to cope with the realization that this was another corridor. It was brightly lit, and there was a scarlet carpet on the floor. Also, it was a short hall, requiring only a few steps before they came to a bigger door, elaborately enscrolled. Ser Perth bent before it, and the door opened silently while he and Dave entered.

The room was large and sparsely furnished. Sitting cross-legged on a cushion near the door was Nema, juggling something in her hands. It looked like a cluster of colored threads, partly woven into a rather garish pattern. On a raised bench between two windows sat the old figure of Sather Karf, resting his chin on hands that held a staff and staring at Dave intently.

Dave stopped as the door closed behind him. Sather Karf nodded, as if satisfied, and Nema tied a complex knot in the threads, then paused silently.

Sather Karf looked far less well than when Dave had last seen him. He seemed older and more shriveled, and there was a querulous, pinched expression in place of the firmness and almost nobility Dave had come to expect. His old eyes bored into the younger man, and he nodded. His voice had a faint quaver now. "All right. You're not much to look at, but you're the best we could find in the Ways we can reach. Come here, Dave Hanson."

The command was still there, however petty the man seemed now. Dave started to phrase some protest, when he found his legs taking him forward to stop in front of Sather Karf, like some clockwork man whose lever has been pushed. He stood in front of the raised bench, noticing that the spot had been chosen to highlight him in the sunset light from the windows. He listened while the old man talked.

Sather Karf began without preamble, stating things in a dry voice as if reading off a list of obvious facts.

"You were dead, Dave Hanson. Dead, buried, and scattered by time and chance until even the place where you lay was forgotten. In your own world, you were nothing. Now you are alive, through the effort of men here whose work you could not even dream of. We have created you, Dave Hanson. Remember that, and forget the ties to any other world, since that world no longer holds you."

Dave nodded slowly. It was hard to swallow, but there were too many things here that couldn't be in any world he had known. And his memory of dying was the clearest memory he had. "All right," he admitted. "You saved my life — or something. And I'll try to remember it. But if this isn't my world, what world is it?"

"The only world, perhaps. It doesn't matter." The old man sighed, and for a moment the eyes were shrouded in speculation, as if he were following some strange by-ways of his own thoughts. Then he shrugged. "It's a world and culture linked to the one you knew only by theories that disagree with each other. And by vision — the vision of those who are adept enough to see through the Ways to the branches of Duality. Before me, there was nothing. But I've learned to open a path — a difficult path for one in this world — and to draw from it, as you have been drawn. Don't try to understand what is a mystery even to the Satheri, Dave Hanson."

"A reasonably intelligent man should be able — " Dave began.

Ser Perth cut his words off with a sharp laugh. "Maybe a man. But who said you were a man, Dave Hanson? Can't you even understand that? You're only half human. The other half is mandrake — a plant that is related to humanity through shapes and signs by magic. We make simulacra out of mandrakes — like the manicurist in the barber shop. And sometimes we use a mandrake root to capture the essence of a real man, in which case he's a mandrake-man, like you. Human? No. But a very good imitation, I must admit."

Dave turned from Ser Perth toward Nema, but her head was bent over the cords she was weaving, and she avoided his eyes. He remembered now that she'd called him a mandrake-man before, in a tone of pity. He looked down at his body, sick in his mind. Vague bits of fairy tales came back to him, suggesting horrible things about mandrake creatures — zombie-like things, only outwardly human.

Sather Karf seemed amused as he looked at Ser Perth. Then the old man dropped his eyes toward Dave, and there was a brief look of pity in them. "No matter, Dave Hanson," he said. "You were human, and by the power of your true name, you are still the same Dave Hanson. We have given you life as precious as your other life. Pay us for that with your service, and that new life will be truly precious. We need your services."

"What do you want?" Dave asked. He couldn't fully believe what he'd heard, but there had been too many strange things to let him disbelieve, either. If they had made him a mandrake-man, then by what little he could remember and guess, they could make him obey them.

"Look out the window — at the sky," Sather Karf ordered.

Dave looked. The sunset colors were still vivid. He stepped forward and peered through the crystalline glass. Before him was a city, bathed in orange and red, towering like the skyline of a dozen cities he had seen — and yet; not like any. The buildings were huge and many-windowed. But some were straight and tall, some were squat and fairy-colored and others blossomed from thin stalks into impossibly bulbous, minareted domes, like long-stemmed tulips reproduced in stone. Haroun-al-Rashid might have accepted the city, but Mayor Wagner could never have believed in it.

"Look at the sky," the old man suggested again, and there was no mockery in his voice now. Dave looked up obediently.

The sunset colors were not sunset. The sun was bright and blinding overhead, surrounded by reddish clouds, glaring down on the fairy city. The sky was — blotchy. It was daylight, but through the clouds bright stars were shining. A corner of the horizon was winter blue; a whole sweep of it was dead, featureless black. It was a nightmare sky, an impossible sky. Dave's eyes bulged as he looked at it.

He turned back to Sather Karf. "What — what's the matter with it?"

"What indeed?" There was bitterness and fear in the old man's voice. In the corner of the room, Nema looked up for a moment, and there was fear and worry in her eyes before she looked back to her weaving of endless knots. Sather Karf sighed in weariness. "If I knew what was happening to the sky, would I be dredging the muck of Duality for the likes of you, Dave Hanson!"

He stood up, wearily but with a certain ease and grace that belied his age, looking down at Dave. There was stern command in his words, but a hint of pleading in his expression.

"The sky's falling, Dave Hanson. Your task is to put it together again. See that you do not fail us!"

He waved dismissal and Ser Perth led Dave and Nema out.

IV

The corridor down which they moved this time was one that might have been familiar even in Dave's Chicago. There was the sound of typewriters from behind the doors, and the floor was covered with composition tile, instead of the too-lush carpets. He began to relax a little until he came to two attendants busily waxing the floor. One held the other by the ankles and pushed the creature's hairy face back and forth, while its hands spread the wax ahead of it. The results were excellent, but Dave found it hard to appreciate.

Ser Perth shrugged slightly. "They're only mandrakes," he explained. He threw open the door of one of the offices and led them through an outer room toward an inner chamber, equipped with comfortable chairs and a desk. "Sit down, Dave Hanson. I'll fill you in on anything you need to know before you're assigned. Now — the Sather Karf told you what you were to do, of course, but — "

"Wait a minute," Dave suggested. "I don't remember being told any such thing."

Ser Perth looked at Nema, who nodded. "He distinctly said you were to repair the sky. I've got it down in my notes if you want to see them." She extended the woven cords.

"Never mind," Ser Perth said. He twiddled with his mustache. "I'll recap a little. Dave Hanson, as you have seen, the sky is falling and must be repaired. You are our best hope. We know that from a prophecy, and it is confirmed by the fact that the fanatics of the Egg have tried several times to kill you. They failed, though one effort was close enough, but their attempts would not have been made at all if they had not been convinced through their arts that you can succeed with the sky."

Dave shook his head. "It's nice to know you trust me!"

"Knowing that you *can* succeed," the other went on smoothly, "we know that you will. It is my unpleasant duty to point out to you the things that will happen if you fail. I say nothing of the fact that you owe us your life; that may be a small enough gift, and one quickly withdrawn. I say only that you have no escape from us. We have your name, and the true symbol is the thing, as you should know. We also have cuttings from your hair and your beard; we have the parings of your nails, five cubic centimeters of your spinal fluid and a scraping from your liver. We have your body through those, nor can you take it out of our reach. Your name gives us your soul." He looked at Hanson piercingly. "Shall I tell you what it would be like for your soul to live in the muck of a swamp in a mandrake root?"

Dave shook his head. "I guess not. I — look, Ser Perth. I don't know what you're talking about. How can I go along with you when I'm in the dark? Start at the beginning, will you? I was killed; all right, if you say I was, I was. You brought me to life again with a mandrake root and spells; you can do anything you want with me. I admit it; right now, I'll admit anything you want me to, because you know what's going on and I don't. But what's all this business of the sky falling? If it is and can be falling, what's the difference? If there is a difference, why should I be able to do anything about it?"

"Ignorance!" Ser Perth murmured to himself. He sighed heavily. "Always ignorance. Well, then, listen." He sat down on the corner of the desk and took out a cigarette. At least it looked like a cigarette. He snapped his fingers and lighted it from a little flame that sprang up, blowing clouds of bright green smoke from his mouth. The smoke hung lazily, drifting into vague patterns and then began to coalesce into a green houri without costume. He swatted at it negligently.

"Dratted sylphs. There's no controlling the elementals properly any more." He didn't seem too displeased, however, as he watched the thing dance off. Then he sobered.

"In your world, Dave Hanson, you were versed in the engineering arts — you more than most. That you should be so ignorant, though you were considered brilliant is a sad commentary on your world. But no matter. Perhaps you can at least learn quickly still. Even you must have had some idea of the composition of the sky?"

Dave frowned as he tried to answer. "Well, I suppose the atmosphere is oxygen and nitrogen, mostly; then there's the ionosphere and the ozone layer. As I remember, the color of the sky is due to the scattering of light — light rays being diffracted in the air."

"Beyond the air," Ser Perth said impatiently. "The sky itself!"

"Oh — space. We were just getting out there with manned ships. Mostly vacuum, of course. Of course, we're still in the solar atmosphere, even there, with the Van Allen belts and such things. Then there are the stars, like our sun, but much more distant. The planets and the moon — "

"Ignorance was bad enough," Ser Perth interrupted in amazement. He stared at Dave, shaking his head in disgust. "You obviously come from a culture of even more superstition than ignorance. Dave Hanson, the sky is no such thing. Put aside the myths you heard as a child. The sky is a solid sphere that surrounds Earth. The stars are no more like the sun than the glow of my cigarette is like a forest fire. They are lights on the inside of the sphere, moving in patterns of the Star Art, nearer to us than the hot lands to the south."

"Fort," Dave said. "Charles Fort said that in a book."

Ser Perth shrugged. "Then why make me say it again? This Fort was right. At least one intelligent man lived in your world, I'm pleased to know. The sky is a dome holding the sun, the stars and the wandering planets. The problem is that the dome is cracking like a great, smashed eggshell."

"What's beyond the dome?"

Ser Perth shuddered slightly. "My greatest wish is that I die before I learn. In your world, had you discovered that there were such things as elements? That is, basic substances which in combination produce — "

"Of course," Dave interrupted.

"Good. Then of the four elements — " Dave gulped, but kept silent, " — of the four elements the universe is built. Some things are composed of a single element; some of two, some of three. The proportions vary and the humors and spirits change but all things are composed of the elements. And only the sky is composed of all four elements — of earth, of water, of fire and of air — in equal proportions. One part each, lending each its own essential quality to the mixture, so that the sky is solid as earth, radiant as fire, formless as water, insubstantial as air. And the sky is cracking and falling, as you have seen for yourself. The effects are already being felt. Gamma radiation is flooding through the gaps; the quick-breeding viruses are mutating through half the world, faster than the Medical Art can control them, so that millions of us are sneezing and choking — and dying, too, for lack of antibiotics and proper care. Air travel is a perilous thing; just today, a stratosphere roc crashed head-on into a fragment of the sky and was killed with all its passengers. Worst of all, the Science of Magic suffers. Because the stars are fixed on the dome of the sky. With the crumbling of that dome, the course of the stars has been corrupted. It's pitiful magic that can be worked without regard to the conjunctions of the planets; but it is all the magic that is left to us. When Mars trines Neptune, the Medical Art is weak; even while we were conjuring you, the trine occurred. It almost cost your life. And it should not have occurred for another seven days."

There was silence, while Ser Perth let Dave consider it. But it was too much to accept at once, and Dave's mind was a treadmill. He'd agreed to admit anything, but some of this was such complete nonsense that his mind rejected it automatically. Yet he was sure Ser Perth was serious; there was no humor on the face of the prissy thin-mustached man before him. Nor had the Sather Karf considered it a joke, he was sure. He had a sudden vision of the latter strangling two men from a distance of thirty feet without touching them. That couldn't happen in a sane world, either.

Dave asked weakly, "Could I have a drink?"

"With a sylph around?" Ser Perth grimaced. "You wouldn't have a chance. Now, is all clear to you, Dave Hanson?"

"Sure. Except for one thing. What am I supposed to do?"

"Repair our sky. It should not be too difficult for a man of your reputation. You built a wall across a continent high and strong enough to change the air currents and affect all your weather — and that in the coldest, meanest country in your world. You come down to us as one of the greatest engineers of history, Dave Hanson, so great that your fame has penetrated even to our world, through the viewing pools of our wisest historians. There is a shrine and monument in your world. 'Dave Hanson, to whom nothing was impossible.' Well, we have a nearly impossible task: a task of engineering and building. If our Science of Magic could be relied upon — but it cannot; it never can be, until the sky is fixed. We have the word of history: no task is impossible to Dave Hanson."

Dave looked at the smug face and a slow grin crept over his own, in spite of himself. "Ser Perth, I'm afraid you've made a slight mistake."

"We don't make mistakes in such matters. You're Dave Hanson," Ser Perth said flatly. "Of all the powers of the Science, the greatest lies in the true name. We evoked you by the name of Dave Hanson. You *are* Dave Hanson, therefore."

"Don't try to deceive us," Nema suggested. Her voice was troubled. "Pray rather that we never have reason to doubt you. Otherwise the wisest of the Satheri would spend their remaining time in planning something unthinkable for you."

Ser Perth nodded vigorous assent. Then he motioned to the office. "Nema will show you to your quarters later. Use this until you leave. I have to report back."

Dave stared after him until he was gone, and then around at the office. He went to the window and stared upwards at the crazy patchwork of the sky. For all he knew, in such a sky there might be cracks. In fact, as he looked, he could make out a rift, and beyond that a ... hole ... a small patch where there was no color, and yet the sky there was not black. There were no stars there, though points of light were clustered around the edges, apparently retreating.

All he had to do was to repair the sky. Shades of Chicken Little!

Maybe to David Arnold Hanson, the famed engineer, no task was impossible. But quite a few things were impossible to that engineer's obscure and unimportant nephew, the computer technician and generally undistinguished man who had been christened Dave. They'd gotten the right man for the name, all right. But the wrong man for the job.

Dave Hanson could repair anything that contained electrical circuits or ran on tiny jeweled bearings, but he could handle almost nothing else. It wasn't stupidity or incapacity to learn, but simply that he had never been subjected to the discipline of construction engineering. Even on the project, while working with his uncle, he had seen little of what went on, and hadn't really understood that, except when it produced data that he could feed into his computer. He couldn't drive a nail in the wall to hang a picture or patch a hole in the plaster.

But it seemed that he'd better put on a good show of trying if he wanted to continue enjoying good health.

"I suppose you've got a sample of the sky that's fallen?" he asked Nema. "And what the heck are you doing here, anyhow? I thought you were a nurse."

She frowned at him, but went to a corner where a small ball of some clear crystalline substance stood. She muttered into it, while a surly face stared out. Then she turned back to him, nodding. "They are sending some of the sky to you. As to my being a nurse, of course I am. All student magicians take up the Medical Art for a time. Surely one so skilled can also be a secretary, even to the great Dave Hanson? As to why I'm here — " She dropped her eyes, frowning, while a touch of added color reached her cheeks. "In the sleep spell I used, I invoked that you should be well and true. But I'm only a bachelor in magic, not even a master, and I slipped. I phrased it that I wanted you well and true. Hence, well and truly do I want you."

"Huh?" He stared at her, watching the blush deepen. "You mean — ?"

"Take care! First you should know that I am proscribed as a duly registered virgin. And in this time of need, the magic of my blood must not be profaned." She twisted sidewise, and then turned toward the door, avoiding him. Before she reached it, the door opened to show a dull clod, entirely naked, holding up a heavy weight of nothing.

"Your sample of sky," she said as the clod labored over to the desk and dropped nothing with a dull clank. The desk top dented slightly.

Dave could clearly see that nothing was on the desk. But if nothing was a vacuum, this was an extremely hard and heavy one. It seemed to be about twelve inches on a side, in its rough shape, and must have weighed two hundred pounds. He tapped it, and it rang. Inside it, a tiny point of light danced frantically back and forth.

"A star," she said sadly.

"I'm going to need some place to experiment with this," he suggested. He expected to be sent to the deepest, dankest cave of all the world as a laboratory, and to find it equipped with pedigreed bats, dried unicorn horns and whole rows of alembics that he couldn't use.

Nema smiled brightly. "Of course. We've already prepared a construction camp for you. You'll find most of the tools you used in your world waiting there and all the engineers we could get or make for you."

He'd been considering stalling while he demanded exactly such things. He was reasonably sure by now that they had no transistors, signal generators, frequency meters or whatever else he could demand. He could make quite an issue out of the need to determine the characteristic impedance of their sky. That might even be interesting, at that; would it be anywhere near 300 ohms here? But it seemed that stalling wasn't going to work. They'd given him what they expected him to need, and he'd have to be careful to need only what they expected, or they might just decide he wasn't Dave Hanson.

"I can't work on this stuff here," he said.

"Then why didn't you say so?" she asked sharply. She let out a cry and a raven came flying in. She whispered something to it, frowned, and then ordered it off. "There's no surface transportation available, and all the local rocs are in use. Well, we'll have to make do with what we have."

She darted for the outer office, rummaged in a cabinet, and came back with a medium-sized rug of worn but gaudy design. Bad imitation Sarouk, Dave guessed. She tossed it onto the largest cleared space, gobbled some outlandish noises, and dropped onto it, squatting near one end. Behind her, the dull clod picked up the sample of sky and fell to his face on the rug. At her vehement signal, Dave squatted down beside her, not daring to believe what he was beginning to guess.

The carpet lifted uncertainly. It seemed to protest at the unbalanced weight of the sky piece. She made the sounds again, and it rose reluctantly, curling up at the front, like a crazy toboggan. It moved slowly, but with increasing speed, sailed out of the office through the window and began gaining altitude. They went soaring over the city at about thirty miles an hour, heading toward what seemed to be barren land beyond. "Sometimes they fail now," she told him. "But so far, only if the words are improperly pronounced."

He gulped and looked gingerly over at the city below. As he did, she gasped. He heard a great tearing sound of thunder. In the sky, a small hole appeared. There was a scream of displaced air, and something went zipping downwards in front of them, setting up a wind that bounced the carpet about crazily. Dave glanced over the edge again to see one of the tall buildings crumple under the impact. The three top stories were ripped to shreds. Then the whole building began to change. It slowly blossomed into a huge cloud of pink gas that rifted away, to show people and objects dropping like stones to the ground below. Nema sighed and turned her eyes away.

"But — it's ridiculous!" Dave protested. "We heard the rip and less than five seconds later, that piece fell. If your sky is even twenty miles above us, it would take longer than that to fall."

"It's a thousand miles up," she told him. "And sky has no inertia until it is contaminated by contact with the ground. It took longer than usual for that piece to fall." She sighed. "It gets worse. Look at the signs. That break has disturbed the planets. We're moving retrograde, back to our previous position, out of Sagittarius! Now we'll go back to the character we had before — and just when I was getting used to the change."

He jerked his eyes off the raw patch of emptiness in the sky, where a few stars seemed to be vanishing. "Your character? Isn't anything stable here?"

"Of course not. Naturally, in each House we have a differing of character, as does the world itself. Why else should astrology be the greatest of the sciences?"

It was a nice world, he decided. And yet the new factor explained some things. He'd been vaguely worried about the apparent change in Ser Perth, who'd turned from a serious and helpful doctor into a supercilious, high-handed fop. But — what about his recovery, if that was supposed to be determined by the signs of the zodiac?

He had no time to ask. The carpet bucked, and the girl began speaking to it urgently. It wavered, then righted itself, to begin sliding downwards.

"There is a ring of protection around your camp," Nema explained. "It is set to make entry impossible to one who does not have the words or who is unfriendly. The carpet could not go through that, anyway. The ring negates all other magic trying to pass it. And of course we have basilisks mounted on posts around the grounds. They're trained to hood their eyes, except when they sense anyone trying to enter who should not. You can't be turned to stone looking at one, you know — only by having one look at you."

"You're cheering me up no end," he assured her.

She smiled pleasantly and began setting the carpet down. Below, he could see a camp that looked much like the camps he had seen in the same movies from which all his clothes had been copied. There were well laid-out rows of sheds, beautiful lines of construction equipment and everything in order, as it could never be in a real camp. As he began walking with the girl toward a huge tent that should have belonged to a circus, he could see other discrepancies. The tractors were designed for work in mud flats and the haulers had the narrow wheels used on rocky ground. Nothing seemed quite as it should be. He spotted a big generator working busily — and then saw a gang of about fifty men, or mandrakes, turning a big capstan that kept it going. Here and there were neat racks of miscellaneous tools. Some were museum pieces. There was even a gandy cart, though no rails for it to run on.

They were almost at the main tent when a crow flew down and yelled something in Nema's ear. She scowled, and nodded. "I'm needed back," she said. "Most of the men here — " She pointed to the gangs that moved about busily doing nothing, all in costumes similar to his, except for the boots and hat. "They're mandrakes, conjured into existence, but without souls. The engineers we have are snatched from Duality just after dying and revived here while their brains still retain their knowledge. They have no true souls either, of course, but they don't know it. Ah. The short man there — he's Garm. Sersa Garm, an apprentice to Ser Perth. He's to be your foreman, and he's real."

She headed back to the outskirts, then turned to shout back. "Sather Karf says you may have ten days to fix the sky," she called. Her hand waved toward him in friendly good-bye. "Don't worry, Dave Hanson. I have faith in you."

Then she was running toward her reluctant carpet.

Dave stared up at the mottled dome above him and at the dull clod — certainly a mandrake — who was still carrying the sample. With all this preparation and a time limit, he couldn't even afford to stall. He'd never fully understood why some plastics melted and others turned hard when heated, but he had to find what was wrong with the dome above and how to fix it. And maybe the time limit could be stretched a little, once he came up with the answer. Maybe. He'd worry about that after he worried about the first steps.

Sersa Garm proved to be a glum, fat young man, overly aware of his importance in training for serhood. He led Dave through the big tent, taking pride in the large drafting section — under the obvious belief that it was used for designing spells. Maybe it could have been useful for that if there had been a single man who knew anything about draftsmanship. There were four engineers, supposedly. One, who had died falling off a bridge while drunk, was curing himself of the shock by remaining dead drunk. One had been a chemical engineer specializing in making yeast and dried soya meal into breakfast cereals. Another knew all about dredging canals and the last one was an electronics engineer — a field in which Dave was far more competent.

He dismissed them. Whatever had been done to them — or perhaps the absence of a true soul, whatever that was — left them rigidly bound to their past ideas and totally incapable of doing more than following orders by routine now. Even Sersa Garm was more useful.

That young man could offer little information, however. The sky, he explained pompously, was a great mystery that only an adept might communicate to another. He meant that he didn't know about it, Dave gathered. Everything, it turned out, was either a mystery or a rumor. He also had a habit of sucking his thumb when pressed too hard for details.

"But you must have heard some guesses about what started the cracks in the sky?" Dave suggested.

"Oh, indeed, that is common knowledge," Sersa Garm admitted. He changed thumbs while he considered. "'Twas an experiment most noble, but through mischance going sadly awry. A great Sather made the sun remain in one place too long, and the heat became too great. It was like the Classic experiment — "

"How hot is your sun?"

There was a long pause. Then Sather Germ shrugged. "'Tis a great mystery. Suffice to say it has no true heat, but does send forth an activating principle against the phlogiston layer, which being excited grows vengeful against the air ... but you have not the training to understand."

"Okay, so they didn't tell you, if they knew." Dave stared up at the sun, trying to guess. The light looked about like what he was used to, where the sky was still whole. North light still was like what a color photographer would consider 5500° Kelvin, so the sun must be pretty hot. Hot enough to melt anything he knew about. "What's the melting point of this sky material?"

He never did manage to make Sather Garm understand what a melting point was. But he found that one of the solutions tried had been the bleeding of eleven certified virgins for seven days. When the blood was mixed with dragonfeathers and frogsdown and melded with a genuine philosopher's stone, they had used it to ink in the right path of the planets of a diagram. It had failed. The sky had cracked and a piece had fallen into the vessel of blood, killing a Sather who was less than two thousand years old.

"Two thousand?" Dave asked. "How old is Sather Karf?"

"None remembers truly. He has always been the Sather Karf — at least ten thousand years or more. To attain the art of a Sather is the work of a score of centuries, usually."

That Sather had been in sad shape, it seemed. No one had been able to revive him, though bringing the dead back to life when the body was reasonably intact was routine magic that even a sersa could perform. It was after that they'd begun conjuring back to Dave's world for all the other experts.

"All whose true names they could find, that is," Garm amended. "The Egyptian pyramid builder, the man who discovered your greatest science, dianetics, the great Cagliostro — and what a time we had finding his true name! I was assigned to the helping of one who had discovered the secrets of gravity and some strange magic which he termed relativity — though indeed it had little to do with kinship, but was a private mystery. But when he was persuaded by divers means to help us, he gave up after one week, declaring it beyond his powers. They were even planning what might best be done to chastise him when he discovered in some manner a book of elementary conjuration and did then devise some strange new formula from the elements with which magic he disappeared."

It was nice to know that Einstein had given up on the problem, Dave thought bitterly. As nice as the discovery that there was no fuel for the equipment here. He spent an hour rigging up a portable saw to use in attempting to cut off a smaller piece of the sky, and then saw the motor burn out when he switched it on. It turned out that all electricity here was d.c., conjured up by commanding the electrons in a wire to move in one direction, and completely useless with a.c. motors. It might have been useful for welding, but there was no electric torch.

"'Tis obviously not a thing of reason," Garm told him severely. "If the current in such a form moves first in one direction and then in the other, then it cancels out and is useless. No, you must be wrong."

As Dave remembered it, Tesla had been plagued by similar doubts from such men as Edison. He gave up and settled finally for one of the native welding torches, filled with a dozen angry salamanders. The flame or whatever it was had enough heat, but it was hard to control. By the time he learned to use it, night had fallen, and he was too tired to try anything more. He ate a solitary supper and went to sleep.

During the next three days he learned a few things the hard way, however. In spite of Garm's assurance that nothing could melt the sky, he found that his sample would melt slowly under the heat of the torch. In the liquid state, it was jet black, though it cooled back to complete transparency. It was also without weight when in liquid form — a fact he discovered when it began rising through the air and spattering over everything, including his bare skin. The burns were nasty, but somehow seemed to heal with remarkable speed. Sersa Garm was impressed by the discoveries, and went off to suck his thumbs and brood over the new knowledge, much to Dave's relief.

More work established the fact that welding bits of the sky together was not particularly difficult. The liquid sky was perfectly willing to bond onto anything, including other bits of itself.

Now, if he could get a gang up the thousand miles to the sky with enough torches to melt the cracks, it might recongeal as a perfect sphere. The stuff was strong, but somewhat brittle. He still had no idea of how to get the stars and planets back in the right places.

"The mathematician thought of such an idea," Sersa Garm said sourly. "But 'twould never work. Even with much heat, it could not be done. For see you, the upper air is filled with phlogiston, which no man can breathe. Also, the phlogiston has negative weight, as every school child must know. Your liquid sky would sink through it, since negative weight must in truth be lighter than no weight, while nothing else would rise through the layer. And phlogiston will quench the flame of a rocket, as your expert von Braun discovered."

The man was a gold mine of information, all bad. The only remaining solution, apparently, was to raise a scaffolding over the whole planet to the sky, and send up mandrakes to weld back the broken pieces. They wouldn't need to breathe, anyhow. With material of infinite strength — and an infinite supply of it — and with infinite time and patience, it might have been worth considering.

Nema came out the next day with more cheering information. Her multi-times great grandfather, Sather Karf, regretted it, but he must have good news to release at once; the populace was starving because the food multipliers couldn't produce reliable supplies. Otherwise, Dave would find venom being transported into his blood in increasing amounts until the pain drove him mad. And, just incidentally, the Sons of the Egg who'd attacked him in the hospital had tried to reach the camp twice already, once by interpenetrating into a shipment of mandrakes, which indicated to what measures they would resort. They meant to kill him somehow, and the defense of him was growing too costly unless there were positive results.

Dave hinted at having nearly reached the solution, giving her only a bit of his wild idea of welding the sky. She took off with that, but he was sure it wouldn't satisfy the Sather. In that, he was right. By nightfall, when she came back from the city, he was groaning in pain. The venom had arrived ahead of her, and his blood seemed to be on fire.

She laid a cool hand on his forehead. "Poor Dave," she said. "If I were not registered and certified, sometimes I feel that I might ... but no more of that. Ser Perth sends you this unguent which will hold back the venom for a time, cautioning you not to reveal his softness." Ser Perth, it seemed, had reverted to his pre-Sagittarian character as expected. "And Sather Karf wants the full plans at once. He is losing patience."

He began rubbing on the ointment, which helped slightly. She peeled back his shirt and began helping, apparently delighted with the hair which he'd sprouted on his chest since his reincarnation. The unguent helped, but it wasn't enough.

"He never had any patience to lose. What the hell does he expect me to do?" Dave asked hotly. "Snap my fingers thus, yell *abracadabra* and give him egg in his beer?"

He stopped to stare at his hand, where a can of beer had suddenly materialized!

Nema squealed in delight. "What a novel way to conjure, Dave. Let me try it." She began snapping her fingers and saying the word eagerly, but nothing happened. Finally she turned back to him. "Show me again."

He was sure it wouldn't work twice, and he hesitated, not too willing to have his stock go down with her. Then he gave in.

"*Abracadabra!*" he said, and snapped his fingers.

There were results at once. This time an egg appeared in his hand, to the delighted cry of Nema. He bent to look at it uncertainly. It was a strange looking egg — more like one of the china eggs used to make hens think they were nesting when their eggs were still being taken from them.

Abruptly Nema sprang back. But she was too late. The egg was growing. It swelled to the size of a football, then was man-sized, and growing to the size of a huge tank that filled most of the tent. Suddenly it split open along one side and a group of men in dull robes and masks came spilling out of it.

"Die!" the one in front yelled. He lifted a double-bladed knife, charged for Dave, and brought the knife down.

The blades went through clothing, skin, flesh and bones, straight for Dave's heart.

V

The knife had pierced Dave's chest until the hilt pressed against his rib cage. He stared down at it, seeing it rise with the heaving of his lungs. Yet he was still alive!

Then the numbness of shock wore off and the pain nerves carried their messages to his brain. He still lived, but there was unholy agony where the blade lay. Coughing and choking on what must be his own blood, he scrabbled at the knife and ripped it out. Blood jetted from the gaping rent in his clothing. It gushed forth — and slowed; it frothed — trickled — and stopped entirely.

As he ripped his shirt back to look, the wound was closed already. But there was no easing of the pain that threatened to make him black out at any second.

He heard shouting, quarreling voices, but nothing made sense through the haze of his agony. He felt someone grab at him — more than one person — and they were dragging him willy-nilly across the ground. Something was clutched around his throat, almost choking him. He opened his eyes just as something clicked behind him.

The huge, translucent walls of the monstrous egg were all around him and the opened side was closing.

The pain began to abate. The bleeding had already stopped entirely and his lungs seemed to have cleared themselves of the blood and froth in them. Now with the ache of the wound ceasing, Dave could still feel the venom burning in his blood, and the constriction around his throat was still there, making it hard to breathe. He sat up, trying to free himself. The constriction came from an arm around his neck, but he couldn't see to whom it belonged, and there was no place to move aside in the corner of the egg.

From inside, the walls of the egg were transparent enough for him to see cloudy outlines of what lay beyond. He could see the ground sweeping away beneath them from all points. A man had run up and was standing beside the egg, beating at it. The man suddenly shot up like a fountain, growing huge; he towered over them, until he seemed miles high and the giant structures Dave could see were only the turned-up toes of the man's shoes. One of those shoes was lifting, as if the man meant to step on the egg.

They must be growing smaller again.

A voice said tightly: "We're small enough, Bork. Can you raise the wind for us now?"

"Hold on." Bork's voice seemed sure of itself.

The egg tilted and soared. Dave was thrown sidewise and had to fight for balance. He stared unbelievingly through the crystal shell. They rose like a Banshee jet. There was a shaggy, monstrous colossus in the distance, taller than the Himalayas — the man who had been beside them. Bork grunted. "Got it! We're all right now." He chanted something in a rapid undertone "All right, relax. That will teach them not to work resonance magic inside a protective ring; the egg knows how we could have got through otherwise. Lucky we were trying at the right time, though. The Satheri must be going crazy. Wait a minute, this tires the fingers."

The man called Bork halted the series of rapid passes he had been making, flexing his fingers with a grimace. The spinning egg began to drop at once, but he let out a long, keening cry, adding a slight flip of his other arm. Outside, something like a mist drew near and swirled around them. It looked huge to Dave, but must have been a small thing in fact. Now they began speeding along smoothly again. The thing was probably another sylph, strong enough to move them in their present reduced size.

Bork pointed his finger. "There's the roc!" He leaned closer to the wall of the tiny egg and shouted. The sylph changed direction, and began to bob about.

It drifted gently, while Bork pulled a few sticks with runes written on them toward him and made a hasty assembly of them. At once, there was a feeling of growing, and the sylph began to shrink away from them. Now they were falling swiftly, growing as they dropped. Dave felt his stomach twist, until he saw they were heading toward a huge bird that was cruising along under them, drawing closer. It looked like a cross between a condor and a hawk, but its wing span must have been over three hundred feet. It slipped under the egg, catching the falling object deftly on a cushion-like attachment between its wings, and then struck off briskly toward the east.

Bork snapped the side of the egg open and stepped out while the others followed. Dave tried to crawl out, but something held him back. It wasn't until Bork's big hand reached in to help him that he made it. When all were out, Bork tapped the egg-shaped object and caught it as it shrank. When it was small enough, he pocketed it.

Dave sat up again, examining himself, now that he had more room. His clothing was a mess, spattered with drying blood, but he seemed unharmed now. Even the burning of the venom was gone. He reached for the arm around his neck and began breaking it free from its stranglehold.

From behind an incredulous cry broke out. Nema sprawled across him, staring at his face and burying her head against his shoulder. "Dave! You're not dead! You're alive!"

Dave was still amazed at that himself. But Bork snorted. "Of course he is. Why'd we take him along with you hanging on in a faint if he were dead? When the snetha-knife kills, it kills completely. They stay dead, or they don't die. Sagittarian?"

She nodded, and the big man seemed to be doing some calculations in his head.

"Yeah," he decided. "It would be. There was one second there around midnight when all the signs were at their absolute maximum favorableness. Someone must have said some pretty dangerous health spells over him then." He turned to Dave, as if aware that the other was comparatively ignorant of such matters. "Happened once before, without this mess-up of the signs. They revived a corpse and found he was unkillable from then on. He lasted eight thousand years, or something like that, before he got burned trying to control a giant salamander. They cut off his head once, but it healed before the axe was all the way through. Woops!"

The bird had dipped downward, rushing toward the ground. It landed at a hundred miles an hour and managed to stop against a small entrance to a cave in the hillside. Except for the one patch where the bird had lighted, they were in the middle of a dense forest.

Dave and Nema were hustled into the cave, while the others melted into the woods, studying the skies. She clung to Dave, crying something about how the Sons of the Egg would torture them.

"All right," he said finally. "Who are these sons of eggs? And what have they got against me?"

"They're monsters," she told him. "They used to be the antimagic individualists. They wanted magic used only when other means wouldn't work. They fought against the Satheri. While magic produced their food and made a better world for them, they hated it because they couldn't do it for themselves. And a few renegade priests like my brother joined them."

"Your brother?"

"She means me," Bork said. He came in to drop on his haunches and grin at Dave. There was no sign of personal hatred in his look. "I used to be a stooge for Sather Karf, before I got sick of it. How do you feel, Dave Hanson?"

Dave considered it, still in wonder at the truth. "I feel good. Even the venom they were putting in my blood doesn't seem to hurt any more."

"Fine. Means the Sather Karf must believe we killed you — he must have the report by now. If he thinks you're dead, there's no point in his giving chase; he knows I wouldn't let them kill Nema, even if she is a little fool. Anyhow, he's not really such a bad old guy, Dave — not, like some of those Satheri. Well, you figure how you'd like it if you were just a simple man and some priest magicked her away from you — and then sent her back with enough magic of her own to be a witch and make life hell for you because she'd been kicked out by the priest, but he hadn't pulled the wanting spell off her. Or anything else you wanted and couldn't keep against magic. Sure, they fed us. They had to, after they took away our fields and the kine, and got everyone into the habit of taking their dole instead of earning our living in the old way. They made slaves of us. Any man who lets another be responsible for him *is* a slave. It's a fine world for the Satheri, if they can keep the egg from breaking."

"What's all this egg nonsense?"

Bork shrugged. "Plain good sense. Why should there be a sky shell around the planet? Look, there's a legend here. You should know it, since for all I know it has some meaning for you. Long ago — or away, or whatever — there was a world called Tharé and another called Erath. Two worlds, separate and distinct, on their own branching time paths. They must have been that way since the moment of creation. One was a world of rule and law. One plus one might not always equal two, but it had to equal something. There seems to be some similarity to your world in that, doesn't there? The other was — well, you'd call it chaos, though it had some laws, if they could be predicted. One plus one there depended — or maybe there was no such thing as unity. Mass-energy wasn't conserved. It was deserved. It was a world of anarchy, from your point of view. It must have been a terrible place to live, I guess."

He hesitated somberly. "As terrible as this one is getting to be," he said at last. "Anyway, there were people who lived there. There were the two inhabited worlds in their own time lines, or probability orbits, or whatever. You know, I suppose, how worlds of probability would separate and diverge as time goes on? Of course. Well, these two worlds *coalesced*."

He looked searchingly at Dave. "Do you see it? The two time lines came together. Two opposites fused into one. Don't ask me to explain it; it was long ago, and all I know for sure is that it happened. The two worlds met and fused, and out of the two came this world, in what the books call the *Dawnstruggle*. When it was over, our world was as it has been for thousands of centuries. In fact, one result was that in theory, neither original world could have a real past, and the fusion was something that had been — no period of change. It's pretty complicated."

"It sounds worse than that," Dave grumbled. "But while that might explain the mystery of magic working here, it doesn't explain your sky."

Bork scratched his head. "No, not too well," he admitted. "I've always had some doubts about whether or not all the worlds have a shell around them. I don't know. But our world does, and the shell is cracking. The Satheri don't like it; they want to stop it. We want it to happen. For the two lines that met and fused into one have an analogue. Doesn't the story of that fusion suggest something to you, Dave Hanson? Don't you see it, the male principle of rule and the female principle of whim; they join, and the egg is fertile! Two universes join, and the result is a nucleus world surrounded by a shell, like an egg. We're a universe egg. And when an egg hatches, you don't try to put it back together!"

He didn't look like a fanatic, Dave told himself. Crazy or not, he took this business of the hatching egg seriously. But you could never be sure about anyone who joined a cult. "What is your egg going to hatch into?" he asked.

The big man shrugged. "Does an egg know it is going to become a hen — or maybe a fish? We can't possibly tell, of course."

Dave considered it. "Don't you even have a guess?"

Bork answered shortly, "No." He looked worried, Dave thought, and guessed that even the fanatics were not quite sure they *wanted* to be hatched. Bork shrugged again.

"An egg has got to hatch," he said. "That's all there is to it. We prophesied this, oh, two hundred years ago. The Satheri laughed. Now they've stopped laughing, but they want to stop it. What happens to a chick when it is stopped from hatching? Does it go on being a chick, or does it die? It dies, of course. And we don't want to die. No, Dave Hanson, we don't know what happens next — but we do know that we must go through with it. I have nothing against you personally — but I can't let you stop us. That's why we tried to kill you. If I could, I'd kill you now, with the snetha-knife so they couldn't revive you."

Dave said reasonably, "You can't expect me to like it, you know. The Satheri, at least, saved my life — " He stopped in confusion. Bork was staring at him in hilarious incredulousness that broke into roars of laughter.

"You mean ... Dave Hanson, do you believe everything they tell you? Don't you know that the Satheri arranged to kill you first? They needed a favorable death conjunction to bring you back to life; they got it — by arranging an accident!"

Nema cried out in protest. "That's a lie!"

"Of course," Bork said mildly. "You always were on their side, little sister. You were also usually a darned nuisance, fond as I was of you. Come here."

He caught her and yanked a single hair out of her head. She screamed and tried to claw him, then fought for the hair. Bork was immovable. He held her off easily with one hand while the fingers of the other danced in the air. He spoke what seemed to be a name, though it bore no resemblance to Nema. She quieted, trembling.

"You'll find a broom near the entrance, little sister. Take it and go back, to forget that Dave Hanson lives. You saw him die and were dragged off with us and his body. You escaped before we reached our hideaway. By the knot I tie in your true hair and by your secret name, this I command."

She blinked slowly and looked around as Bork burned the knotted hair. Her eyes swept past Bork and Dave without seeing them and centered on the broom one man held out to her, without appearing to see him, either. She seized the broom. A sob came to her throat. "The devil! The renegade devil! He didn't have to kill Dave! He didn't — "

Her voice died away as she ran toward the clearing. Dave made no protest. He suspected Bork was putting the spell on her for her own good, and he agreed that she was better out of all this.

"Now where were we?" Bork asked. "Oh, yes, I was trying to convert you and knowing I'd failed already. Of course, I don't know that they killed you first — but those are their methods. Take it from me, I know. I was the youngest Ser ever to be accepted for training as a Sather. They wanted you, so they got you."

Dave considered it. It seemed as likely as anything else. "Why me?" he asked.

"Because you can put back the sky. At least, the Satheri think so, and I must admit that in some ways they are smarter than we."

Dave started to protest, but Bork cut him off.

"I know all about your big secret. You're not the engineer, whose true name was longer. We know all that. Our pools are closer to perfection than theirs, not being contaminated by city air, and we see more. But there is a cycle of confirmation; if prophecy indicates a thing will happen, it will happen — though not always as expected. The prophecy fulfills itself, rather than being fulfilled. Then there are the words on the monument — a monument meant for your uncle, but carrying your true name, because his friends felt the short form sounded better. It was something of a coincidence that they had the wrong true name. But prophecy is always strongest when based on coincidence — that is a prime rule. And those words coupled with our revelations prophesy that *you* — not your uncle — can do the impossible. So what are we going to do with you?"

Bork's attitude was reassuring, somehow. It was nearer his own than any Dave had heard on this world. And the kidnapping was beginning to look like a relief. The Sons of the Egg had gotten him off the hook with Sather Karf. He grinned and stretched back. "If I'm unkillable, Bork, what can you do?"

The big man grinned back. "Flow rock around you up to your nose and toss you into a lake. You'd live there — but you'd always be drowning and you'd find it slightly unpleasant for the next few thousand years! It's not as bad as being turned into a mangrove with your soul intact, but it would last longer. And don't think the Satheri can't pull a lot worse than that. They have your name — everyone has your secret name here — and parts of you."

The conversation was suddenly less pleasant. Dave thought it over. "I could stay here and join your group. I might as well, since I can't really help the Satheri anyhow."

"They'd spot your aura eventually. They'll be checking around here for us for a while. Of course, we might do something about it, if you really converted. But I don't think you would, if you knew more." Bork got up and headed for the entrance. "I wasn't going to let you see the risings, but now maybe I will. If you still want to join, it might be worked. Otherwise, I'll think of something else."

Dave followed the man out into the clearing. A few men were just planning to leave, and they looked at Dave suspiciously, but made no protest. One, whom Dave recognized as the leader with the snetha-knife, scowled.

"The risings are almost due, Bork," he said.

Bork nodded. "I know, Malok. I've decided to let Dave Hanson watch. Dave, this is our leader here, Res Malok."

Dave felt no strong love for his would-be murderer, and it seemed to be mutual. But no protest was lodged. Apparently Bork was their top conjurer, and privileged. They crossed the clearing and went through the woods toward another, smaller one. Here a group of some fifty men were watching the sky, obviously waiting. Others stood around, watching them and avoiding looking up. Almost directly overhead, there was a rent place where the strange absence of color or feature indicated a hole in the dome over them. As it drew nearer true vertical, a chanting began among the men with up-turned faces. Their hands went upwards, fingers spread and curled into an unnatural position. Then they stood waiting.

"I don't like it," Bork whispered to Dave. "This is one of the reasons we're growing too weak to fight the Satheri."

"What's wrong with a ceremony of worship, if you must worship your eggshell?" Dave asked.

"You'll see. That was all it was once — just worship. But now for weeks, things are changing. They think it's a sign of favor, but I don't know. There, watch!"

The hole in the sky was directly overhead now, and the moaning had risen in pitch. Across the little clearing, Malok began backing quietly away, carefully not looking upwards. Nobody but Dave seemed to notice his absence. There was a louder moan.

One of the men in the clearing began to rise upwards slowly. His body was rigid as it lifted a foot, ten feet, then a hundred above the ground. Now it picked up speed, and rushed upwards. Another began to rise, and another. In seconds, more than half of those who had waited were screaming upwards toward the hole in the sky. They disappeared in the distance.

Those who had merely stood by and those who had worshipped waited a few seconds more, but no more rose. The men sighed and began moving out of the clearing. Dave arose to follow, but Bork gestured for him to wait.

"Sometimes — " he said.

They were alone now. Still Bork waited, staring upwards. Then Dave saw something in the sky. A speck appeared and came hurtling down. In seconds, it was the body of one of the men who had risen. Dave felt his stomach tighten and braced himself. There was no slowing as the body fell. It landed in the center of the clearing, without losing speed, but with less noise than he had expected.

When they reached the shattered body, there could be no question of its being dead.

Bork's face was solemn. "If you're thinking of joining, you'd better know the worst. You're too easily shocked to make a good convert unless you're prepared. The risings have been going on for some time. Malok swears it proves we are right. But I've seen five other bodies come down like this. What does it mean? Are they stillborn? We don't know. Shall I revive him for you?"

Dave felt sick as he stared at the ghastly terror on the face of the corpse. The last thing he wanted to see was its revival, but his curiosity about the secret in the sky could not be denied. He nodded.

Bork drew a set of phials and implements in miniature size from under his robe. "This is routine," he said. He snapped his fingers and produced a small flame over the heart of the corpse. Into that he began dusting powders, mixing them with something that looked like blood. Finally he called a name and a command. There was a sharp explosion, a hissing, and Bork's voice calling.

The dead man flowed together and was whole. He stood up woodenly, with his face frozen. "Who calls?" he asked in an uninflected, hollow voice. "Why am I called? I have no soul."

"We call," Bork answered. "Tell us what you saw at the hole in the sky."

A scream tore from the throat of the thing, and its hands came up to its eyes, tearing at them. Its mouth worked soundlessly, and breath sucked in. Then a single word came out.

"Faces!"

It fell onto the grass, distorted in death again. Bork shuddered.

"The others were the same," he said. "And he can't be revived again. Even the strongest spell can't bring back his soul. That is gone, somehow."

Dave shivered. "And knowing that, you'd still fight against repairing the sky?"

"Hatching is probably always horrible from inside the shell," Bork answered. "Do you still want to join us? No, I thought not. Well, then, let's go back. We might as well try to eat something while I think about what to do with you."

Malok and most of the others were gone when they reached the cave again. Bork fell to work with some scraps of food, cursing the configurations of the planets as his spell refused to work. Then suddenly the scraps became a mass of sour-smelling stuff. Bork made a face as he tasted it, but he ate it in silence. Dave couldn't force himself to put it in his mouth, though he was hungry by then.

He considered, and then snapped his fingers. "Abracadabra," he cried. He swore as something wet and slimy that looked like seaweed plopped into his hand. The next time he got a limp fish that had been dead far too long. But the third try worked better. This time, a whole bunch of bananas appeared. They were a little riper than he liked, but some of them were edible enough. He handed some to the other man, who quickly abandoned his own creation.

Bork was thoughtful as he ate. Finally he grimaced. "New magic!" he said. "Maybe that's the secret of the prophecy. I thought you knew no magic."

"I didn't," Dave admitted. He was still tingling inside himself at this confirmation of his earlier discovery. It was unpredictable magic, but apparently bore some vague relationship to what he was wishing for.

"So the lake's out," Bork decided. "With unknown powers at your command, you might escape in time. Well, that settles it. There's one place where nobody will look for you or listen to you. You'll be nothing but another among millions, and that's probably the best hiding place for you. With the overseers they have, you couldn't even turn yourself back to the Satheri, though I'll admit I'm hoping you don't want them to find you."

"And I was beginning to think you liked me," Dave commented bitterly.

Bork grinned. "I do, Dave Hanson. That's why I'm picking the easiest place to hide you I can think of. It will be hell, but anything else would be worse. Better strip and put this cloth on."

The thing he held out was little more than a rag, apparently torn from one of the robes. "Come on, strip, or I'll burn off your clothes with a salamander. There, that's better. Now wrap the cloth around your waist and let it hang down in front. It'll be easier on you if you don't attract much attention. The sky seems to indicate the planets favor teleportation now. Be quick before I change my mind and think of something worse!"

Dave didn't see what he did this time, but there was a puff of flame in front of his eyes.

The next second, he stood manacled in a long line of men loaded with heavy stones. Over their backs fell the cutting lashes of a whip. Far ahead was a partially finished pyramid. Dave was obviously one of the building slaves.

VI

Sunrise glared harshly over the desert. It was already hot enough to send heat waves dancing over the sand as Hanson wakened under the bite of a lash. The overseers were shouting and kicking the slaves awake. Overhead the marred sky shone in crazy quilt patterns.

Hanson stood up, taking the final bite of the whip without flinching. He glanced down at his body, noticing that it had somehow developed a healthy deep tan during the few hours of murderous labor the day before. He wasn't particularly surprised. Something in his mind seemed also to have developed a "tan" that let him face the bite of chance without flinching. He'd stopped wondering and now accepted; he meant to get away from here at the first chance and he was somehow sure he could.

It was made easier by the boundless strength of his new body. He showed no signs of buckling under physical work that would have killed him on his own world.

Not all the slaves got up. Two beside him didn't move at all. Sleeping through that brutal awakening seemed impossible. When Hanson looked closer, he saw that they weren't asleep; they were dead.

The overseer raged back along the line and saw them. He must be one of those conjured into existence here from the real Egypt of the past. He might have no soul, but a lifetime of being an overseer had given him habits that replaced the need for what had been a pretty slim soul to begin with.

"Quitters!" he yelled. "Lazy, worthless, work-dodging goldbrick artists!" He knelt in fury, thumbing back the eyelids of the corpses. There was little need for the test. They were too limp, too waxen to be pretending.

The overseer cut them out of the chain and kicked at Hanson. "Move along!" he bellowed. "Menes himself is here, and he's not as gentle as I am."

Hanson joined the long line, wondering what they were going to do about breakfast. How the devil did they expect the slaves to put in sixteen hours of work without some kind of food? There had been nothing the night before but a skin of water. There was not even that much this morning. No wonder the two beside him had died from overwork, beatings and plain starvation.

Menes was there, all right. Hanson saw him from the distance, a skinny giant of a man in breechclout, cape and golden headdress. He bore a whip like everyone else who seemed to have any authority at all, but he wasn't using it. He was standing hawklike on a slight rise in the sandy earth, motionless and silent. Beside him was a shorter figure: a pudgy man with a thin mustache, on whom the Egyptian headdress looked strangely out of place. It could only be Ser Perth!

Hanson's staring came to an end as the lash cut down across his shoulders, biting through to the shoulder-bone. He stumbled forward, heedless of the overseers' shouting voices. Someday, if he had the chance, he'd flay his own overseer, but that could wait. Even the agony of the cut couldn't take his mind from Ser Perth's presence. Had Bork slipped up — did the Satheri know that Hanson was still alive, and had they sent Ser Perth here to locate him? It seemed unlikely, however. The man was paying no attention to the lines of slaves. It would be hard to spot one among three million, anyhow. More likely, Hanson decided, Ser Perth was supervising the supervisors, making an inspection tour of all this.

Of all what? Apparently then this must be another of their frenzied efforts to find a way to put back the sky. He'd heard that they had called up the pyramid builder, but hadn't fully realized it would lead to this type of activity.

He looked around him appraisingly. The long lines of slaves that had been carrying rock and rubble the day before now were being formed into hauling teams. Long ropes were looped around enormous slabs of quarried rock. Rollers underneath them and slaves tugging and pushing at them were the only means of moving them. The huge stones slid remorselessly forward onto the prepared beds of rubble. Casting back in his memory, Hanson could not recall seeing the rock slabs the night before. They had appeared as if by magic —

Obviously, they had really been conjured up by magic. But if the rocks could be conjured, what was the need of all the slaves and the sadistic overseers? Why not simply magic the entire construction, whatever it was to be?

The whip hit him again, and the raging voice of the overseer ranted in his ears. "Get on, you blundering slacker. Menes himself is looking at you. Ho there — what the devil?"

The overseer's hand spun Hanson around. The man's eyes, large and opaque, stared at Hanson. He frowned cruelly. "Yeah, you're the same one! Didn't I take the hide off your back twice already? And now you stand there without a scar or a drop of blood!"

Hanson grunted feebly. He didn't want attention called to himself while Ser Perth was around. "I — I heal quickly." It was no more than the truth. Either the body they'd given him or the conjuring during the right split second had enabled him to heal almost before a blow was struck.

"Magic!" The overseer scowled and gave Hanson a shove that sent him sprawling. "Blithering magic again! Magic stones that melt when you get them in place — magic slaves that the whip won't touch! And they expect us to do a job of work such as not even Thoth could dream up! They won't take honest work. No, they have to come snooping and conjuring and interfering. Wheels on rollers! Tools of steel and the gods know what instead of honest stone. Magic to lift things instead of honest ropes that shrink and wood that swells. Magic that fails, and rush, rush, rush until I'm half ready to be tortured for falling behind, and — you! You would, would you!" His voice trailed off into a fresh roar of rage as he caught sight of other slaves taking advantage of his attention to Hanson to relax. He raced off, brandishing the whip.

Hanson tried to make himself inconspicuous after that. The wounds would heal, and the beatings could never kill him; but there had been no provision in his new body for the suppression of pain. He hungered, thirsted and suffered like anyone else. Maybe he was learning to take it, here, but not to like it.

At the expense of a hundred slaves and considerable deterioration of the whips, one block of stone was in place before the sun was high overhead in the coppery, mottled sky. Then there was the blessing of a moment's pause. Men were coming down the long lines, handing something to the slaves. Food, Hanson anticipated.

He was wrong. When the slave with the wicker basket came closer he could see that the contents were not food but some powdery stuff that was dipped out with carved spoons into the eager hands of the slaves. Hanson smelled his portion dubiously. It was cloying, sickly sweet.

Hashish! Or opium, heroin, hemp — Hanson was no expert. But it was certainly some kind of drug. Judging by the avid way the other slaves were gulping it down, each one of them had been exposed to it before. Hanson cautiously made the pretense of swallowing his before he allowed it to slip through his fingers to mingle with the sand. Drug addiction was obviously a convenient way to make the slaves forget their aches and fears, to keep them everlasting anxious to please whatever was necessary to make sure the precious, deadly ration never stopped.

There was still no sign of food. The pause in the labor was only for the length of time it took the drug-bearing slaves to complete their task. Ten minutes, or fifteen at the outside; then the overseers were back with the orders and the lashes.

The slaves regrouped on new jobs, and Hanson found himself in a bunch of a dozen or so. They were lashing the hauling ropes around a twelve-foot block of stone; the rollers were already in place, with the crudely plaited ropes dangling loosely. Hanson found himself being lifted by a couple of the other slaves to the shoulders of a third. His clawing hands caught the top of the block and the slaves below heaved him upward. He scrambled to the top and caught the ropes that were flung up to him.

From his vantage point he saw what he had not seen before — the amazing size of the construction project. This was no piffling little Gizeh pyramid, no simple tomb for a king. Its base was measured in kilometers instead of yards, and its top was going to be proportionally high, apparently. It hardly seemed that there could be enough stone in the whole world to finish the job. As far as Hanson could see, over the level sand, the ground was black with the suffering millions of slaves in their labor gangs.

The idiots must be trying to reach the sky with their pyramid. There could be no other answer to the immense bulk planned for this structure. Like the pride-maddened men of Babel, they were building a sky-high thing of stone. It was obviously impossible, and even Menes must be aware of that. Yet perhaps it was no more impossible than all the rest of the things in this impossible world.

When the warlocks of this world had discovered that they could not solve the problem of the sky, they must have gone into a state of pure hysteria, like a chicken dashing back and forth in front of a car. They had sought through other worlds and ages for anyone with a reputation as a builder, engineer or construction genius, without screening the probability of finding an answer. The size of the ancient pyramid must have been enough to sway them. They had used Hanson, Menes, Einstein, Cagliostro — for some reason of their own, since he'd never been a builder — and probably a thousand more. And then they had half-supplied all of them, rather than picking the most likely few and giving full cooperation. Magic must have made solutions to most things so easy that they no longer had the guts to try the impossible themselves. A pyramid seemed like a ridiculous solution, but for an incredible task, an impossible solution had to be tried.

And maybe, he thought, they'd overlooked the obvious in their own system. The solution to a problem in magic should logically be found in magic, not in the methods of other worlds. His mind groped for something that almost came into his consciousness — some inkling of what should have been done, or how they had failed. It was probably only an idle fancy, but —

"Hey!" One of the slaves below was waving at him. While Hanson looked down, the slave called to another, got a shoulder to lean on, and walked his way up the side of the block, pushed from below and helped by Hanson's hands above. He was panting when he reached the top, but he could still talk. "Look, it's your skin, but you're going to be in trouble if you don't get busy. Look out for that overseer up there. Don't just stand around when he's in sight." He picked up a loop of rope and passed it to Hanson, making a great show of hard work.

Hanson stared up at the overseer who was staring back at him. "Why is he any worse than the rest of this crowd?"

The slave shuddered as the dour, slow-moving overseer began walking stiffly toward them. "Don't let the fact that he's an overseer fool you. He's smarter than most of his kind, but just as ugly. He's a mandrake, and you can't afford to mess with him."

Hanson looked at the ancient, wrinkled face of the mandrake and shuddered. There was the complete incarnation of inhumanity in the thing's expression. He passed ropes around the corners until the mandrake turned and rigidly marched away, the blows of his whip falling metronome-like on the slaves he passed. "Thanks," Hanson said "I wonder what it's like, being a true mandrake?"

"Depends," the slave said easily. He was obviously more intelligent than most, and better at conserving himself. "Some mandrake-men are real. I mean, the magicians want somebody whom they can't just call back — direct translation of the body usually messes up the brain patterns enough to make the thinkers hard to use, especially with the sky falling. So they get his name and some hold on his soul and then rebuild his body around a mandrake root. They bind his soul into that, and in some ways he's almost human. Sometimes they even improve on what he was. But the true mandrake — like that one — never was human. Just an ugly, filthy simulacrum. It's bad business. I never liked it, even though I was in training for sersa rating."

"You're from this world?" Hanson asked in surprise. He'd been assuming that the man was one of the things called back.

"A lot of us are. They conscripted a lot of the people they didn't need for these jobs. But I was a little special. All right, maybe you don't believe me — you think they wouldn't send a student sersa here now. Look, I can prove it. I managed to sneak one of the books I was studying back with me. See?"

He drew a thin volume from his breechclout cautiously, then slipped it back again. "You don't get such books unless you're at least of student rating." He sighed, then shrugged. "My trouble is that I could never keep my mouth shut. I was attendant at one of the revivatoria, and I got drunk enough to let out some information about one of the important revival cases. So here I am."

"Umm." Hanson worked silently for a minute, wondering how far coincidence could go. It could go a long ways here, he decided. "You wouldn't have been sentenced to twenty lifetimes here by the Sather Karf, would you?"

The slave stared at him in surprise. "You guessed it. I've died only fourteen times so far, so I've got six more lives to go. But — hey, you can't be! They were counting on you to be the one who really fixed things. Don't tell me my talking out of turn did this to you."

Hanson reassured him on that. He recognized the man now for another reason. "Aren't you the one I saw dead on his back right next to me this morning?"

"Probably. Name's Barg." He stood up to take a careful look at the net of cording around the stone. "Looks sound enough. Yeah, I died this morning, which is why I'm fairly fresh now. Those overseers won't feed us because it takes time and wastes food; they let us die and then have us dragged back for more work. It's a lot easier on the ones they dragged back already dead; dying doesn't matter so much without a soul."

"Some of them seem to be Indians," Hanson noted. He hadn't paid too much attention, but the slaves seemed to be from every possible background.

Barg nodded. "Aztecs from a place called Tenochtitlan. Twenty thousand of them got sacrificed in a bunch for some reason or other. Poor devils. They think this is some kind of heaven. They tell me this is easy work compared to the type they had to undergo. The Satheri like to get big bunches through in one conjuration, like the haul they made from the victims of somebody named Tamerlane." He tested a rope, then dropped to a sitting position on the edge of the block. "I'll let you stay up to call signals from here. Only watch it. That overseer has his eyes on you. Make sure the ropes stay tight while we see if the thing can be moved."

He started to slip over the side, hanging by his fingertips. Something caught, and he swore. With one hand, he managed to free his breechclout and drag out the thin volume that was lodged between his groin and the block. "Here, hold this for me until we meet tonight. You've got more room to hide it in your cloth than I have." He tossed it over quickly, then dropped from sight to land on the ground below.

Hanson shoved the book out of sight and tried to act busy again. The mandrake overseer had started ponderously toward him. But in a moment the thing's attention was directed to some other object of torture.

Hanson braced himself as the lines of slaves beneath him settled themselves to the ropes. There was a loud cracking of whips and a chorus of groans. A small drum took up a beat, and the slaves strained and tugged in unison. Ever so slowly, the enormous block of stone began to move, while the ropes drew tighter.

Hanson checked the rigging with half his mind, while the other half raced in a crazy circle of speculation. Mandrakes and mandrake-men, zombie-men, from the past and multiple revivals! A sky that fell in great chunks. What came next in this ridiculous world in which he seemed to be trapped?

As if in answer to his question, there was a sudden, coruscating flare from above.

Hanson's body reacted instinctively. His arm came up over his eyes, cutting off the glare. But he managed to squint across it, upwards toward what was happening in the cracked dome. For a split second, he thought that the sun had gone nova.

He was wrong, but not by too much. Something had happened to the sun. Now it was flickering and flaming, shooting enormous jets of fire from its rim. It hovered at the edge of a great new hole and seemed to be wobbling, careening and losing its balance.

There was a massive shriek of fear and panic from the horde of slaves. They began bellowing like the collective death-agony of a world. Most of them dropped their ropes and ran in blind panic, trampling over each other in their random flight for safety. The human overseers were part of the same panic-stricken riot. Only the mandrakes stood stolidly in place, flicking each running man who passed them.

Hanson flung himself face down on the stone. There was a roar of tortured air from overhead and a thundering sound that was unlike anything except the tearing of an infinity of cloth combined with a sustained explosion of atomic bombs. Then it seemed as if the thunderbolt of Thor himself had blasted in Hanson's ears.

The sky had ripped again, and this time the entire dome shook with the shock. But that wasn't the worst of it.

The sun had broken through the hole and was falling!

VII

The fall of the sun was seemingly endless. It teetered out of the hole and seemed to hover, spitting great gouts of flame as it encountered the phlogiston layer. Slowly, agonizingly, it picked up speed and began its downward rush. Unlike the sky, it seemed to obey the normal laws of inertia Hanson had known. It swelled bit by bit, raging as it drew nearer. And it seemed to be heading straight for the pyramid.

The heat was already rising. It began to sear the skin long before the sun struck the normal atmosphere. Hanson could feel that he was being baked alive. The blood in his arteries seemed to bubble and boil, though that must have been an illusion. But he could see his skin rise in giant blisters and heal almost at once to blister again. He screamed in agony, and heard a million screams around him. Then the other screams began to decrease in numbers and weaken in volume, and he knew that the slaves were dying.

Through a slit between two fingers, he watched the ponderous descent. The light was enough to sear his retinas, but even they healed faster than the damage. He estimated the course of the sun, amazed to find that there was no panic in him, and doubly amazed that he could think at all over the torture that wracked his body.

Finally, convinced that the sun would strike miles to the south, he rolled across the scorching surface of the stone block and dropped to the north side of it. The shock of landing must have broken bones, but a moment later he could begin to breathe again. The heat was still intense, even behind the stone block, but it was bearable — at least for him.

Pieces were breaking off the sun as it fell, and already striking the ground. One fell near, and its heat seared at him, giving him no place of shelter. Then the sun struck, sending up earth tremors that knocked him from his feet. He groped up and stared around the block.

The sun had struck near the horizon, throwing up huge masses of material. Its hissing against the ground was a tumult in his ears, and superheated ash and debris began to fall.

So far as he could see, there were no other survivors in the camp. Three million slaves had died. Those who had found some shelter behind the stonework had lived longer than the others, but that had only increased their suffering. And even his body must have been close to its limits, if it could be killed at all.

He was still in danger. If a salamander could destroy even such a body as his, then the fragments of sun that were still roiling across the landscape would be fatal. The only hope he had was to get as far away from the place where the sun had struck as he could.

He braced himself to leave even the partial shelter. There was a pile of water skins near the base of the block, held in the charred remains of an attendant's body. The water was boiling, but there was still some left. He poured several skins together and drank the stuff, forcing himself to endure the agony of its passage down his throat. Without it, he'd be dehydrated before he could get a safe distance away.

Then he ran. The desert was like molten iron under his bare feet, and the savage radiation on his back was worse than any overseer's whip. His mind threatened to blank out with each step, but he forced himself on. And slowly, as the distance increased, the sun's pyre sank further and further over the horizon. The heat should still have been enough to kill any normal body in fifteen minutes, but he could endure it. He stumbled on in a trot, guiding himself by the stars that shone in the broken sky toward a section of this world where there had been life and some measure of civilization before. After a few hours, the tongues of flame no longer flared above the horizon, though the brilliant radiance continued. And Hanson found that his strong and nearly indestructible body still had limits. It could not go on without rest forever. He was sobbing with fatigue at every step.

He managed to dig a small hollow in the sand before dropping off to sleep. It was a sleep of total exhaustion, lacking even a sense of time. It might have been minutes or hours that he slept, and he had no way of knowing which. With the sun gone and the stars rocking into dizzy new configurations, there was no night or day, nor any way to guess the passage of time.

He woke to a roaring wind that sent cutting blasts of sand driving against him. He staggered up and forced himself against it, away from the place where the sun had fallen. Even through the lashing sandstorm, he could see the glow near the horizon. Now a pillar of something that looked like steam but was probably vapor from molten and evaporated rocks was rising upwards, like the mushroom clouds of his own days. It was spreading, apparently just under the phlogiston layer, reflecting back the glare. And the wind was caused by the great rising column of superheated gases over the sun.

He staggered on, while the sand gave way slowly to patches of green. With the sun gone and the sky falling into complete shreds, this world was certainly doomed. He'd assumed that the sun of this world must be above the sky, but he'd been wrong; like the other heavenly bodies, it had been embedded inside the shell. He had discovered that the sky material resisted any sudden stroke, but that other matter could be interpenetrated into it, as the stars were. He had even been able to pass his hand and arm completely through the sample. Apparently the sun had passed through the sky in a similar manner.

Then why hadn't the shell melted? He had no real answer. The sun must have been moving fast enough so that no single spot became too hot, or else the phlogiston layer somehow dissipated the heat.

The cloud of glowing stuff from the rising air column was spreading out now, reflecting the light and heat back to the earth. There was a chance that most of one hemisphere might retain some measure of warmth, then. At least there was still light enough for him to travel safely.

By the time he was too tired to go on again, he had come to the beginnings of fertile land. He passed a village, but it had been looted, and he skirted around it rather than stare at the ghastly ghoul-work of the looters. The world was ending, but civilization seemed to have ended already. Beyond it, he came to a rude house, now abandoned. He staggered in gratefully.

For a change, he had one piece of good luck. His first attempt at magic produced food. At the sound of the snapping fingers and his hoarse-voiced "abracadabra," a dirty pot of hot and greasy stew came into existence. He had no cutlery, but his hands served well enough. When it was gone, he felt better. He wiped his hands on the breechclout. Whatever the material in the cloth, it had stood the sun's heat almost as well as he had.

Then he paused as his hand found a lump under the cloth. He drew out the apprentice magician's book. The poor devil had never achieved his twenty lifetimes, and this was probably all that was left of him. Hanson stared at it, reading the title in some surprise.

Applied Semantics.

He propped himself up and began to scan it, wondering what it had to do with magic. He'd had a course of semantics in college and could see no relationship. But he soon found that there were differences.

This book began with the axiomatic statement that the symbol is the thing. From that it developed in great detail the fact that any part of a whole bearing similarity to the whole was also the whole; that each seven was the class of all sevens; and other details of the science of magical similarity followed quite logically from the single axiom. Hanson was surprised to find that there was a highly developed logic to it. Once he accepted the axiom — and he was no longer prepared to doubt it here — he could follow the book far better than he'd been able to follow his own course in semantics. Apparently this was supposed to be a difficult subject, from the constant efforts of the writer to make his point clear. But after learning to deal with electron holes in transistors, this was elementary study for Hanson.

The second half of the book dealt with the use of the true name. That, of course, was the perfect symbol, and hence the true whole. There was the simple ritual of giving a secret name. Apparently any man who discovered a principle or device could use a name for it, just as parents could give one to their children. And there were the laws for using the name. Unfortunately, just when Hanson was beginning to make some sense of it, the book ended. Obviously, there was a lot more to be covered in later courses.

He tossed the book aside, shivering as he realized that his secret name was common knowledge. The wonder was that he could exist at all. And while there was supposed to be a ritual for relinquishing one name and taking another, that was one of the higher mysteries not given.

In the morning, he stopped to magic up some more food and the clothing he would need if he ever found the trace of civilized people again. The food was edible, though he'd never particularly liked cereal. He seemed to be getting the hang of abracadabraing up what was in his mind. But the clothing was a problem. Everything he got turned out to be the right size, but he couldn't see himself in hauberk and greaves, nor in a filmy nightgown. Finally, he managed something that was adequate, if the brilliant floral sportshirt could be said to go with levi pants and a morning frock. But he felt somewhat better in it. He finally left the frock behind, however. It was still too hot for that.

He walked on briskly, watching for signs of life and speculating on the principles of applied semantics, name magic and similarity. He could begin to understand how an Einstein might read through one of the advanced books here and make leaps in theory beyond what the Satheri had developed. They'd had it too easy. Magic that worked tended to overcome the drive for the discipline needed to get the most out of it. Any good theoretician from Hanson's world could probably make fools of these people. Maybe that was why the Satheri had gone scrounging back through other worlds to find men who had the necessary drive to get things done when the going was tough.

Twice he passed abandoned villages, but there was nothing there for him. He was coming toward forested ground now, something like the country in which the Sons of the Egg had found refuge. The thought of that made him go slower. But for a long time, there was no further sign of life. The woods thinned out to grasslands, and he went on for hours more before he spotted a cluster of lights ahead.

As he drew nearer, he saw that the lights seemed to be fluorescents. They were coming from corrugated iron sheds that looked like aircraft hangars strung together. There was a woven-wire fence around the structures, and a sign that said simply: *Project Eighty-Five*. In the half-light from the sky, he could see a well-kept lawn, and there were a few groups of men standing about idly. Most wore white coveralls, though two were dressed in simple business suits.

Hanson moved forward purposefully, acting as if he had urgent business. If he stopped, there would be questions, he suspected; he wanted to find answers, not to answer idle questions.

There was no one at the desk in the little reception alcove, but he heard the sound of voices through a side door leading out. He went through it, to find a larger yard with more men idling. There should be someone here who knew more of what was going on in this world than he did now.

His choice, in the long run, seemed to lie between Bork and the Satheri, unless he could find some way of hiding himself from both sides. At the moment, he was relatively free for the first time since they had brought him here, and he wanted to make sure that he could make the most use of the fact.

Nobody asked anything. He slowed, drifting along the perimeter of the group of men, and still nobody paid him any attention. Finally, he dropped onto the ground near a group of half a dozen men who looked more alert than the rest. They seemed to be reminiscing over old times.

" — two thirty-eight an hour with overtime — and double time for the swing shift. We really had it made then! And every Saturday, never fail, the general would come out from Muroc and tell us we were the heros of the home front — with overtime pay while we listened to him!"

"Yeah, but what if you wanted to quit? Suppose you didn't like your shift boss or somebody? You go down and get your time, and they hand you your draft notice. Me, I liked it better in '46. Not so much pay, but — "

Hanson pricked up his ears. The conversation told him more than he needed to know. He stood up and peered through the windows of the shed. There, unattended under banks of lights, stood half-finished aircraft shapes.

He wouldn't get much information here, it seemed. These were obviously reanimates, men who'd been pulled from his own world and set to work. They could do their duties and their memories were complete, but they were lacking some essential thing that had gone out of them before they were brought here. Unless he could find one among them who was either a mandrake-man housing a soul or one of the few reanimates who seemed almost fully human, he'd get little information. But he was curious as to what the Satheri had expected to do with aircraft. The rocs had better range and altitude than any planes of equal hauling power.

He located one man who seemed a little brighter than the others. The fellow was lying on the ground, staring at the sky with his hands clasped behind his head. From time to time, he frowned, as if the sight of the sky was making him wonder. The man nodded as Hanson dropped down beside him. "Hi. Just get here, Mac?"

"Yeah," Hanson assented. "What's the score?"

The man sat up and made a disgusted noise. "Who knows?" he answered. There was more emotion in his voice than might be expected from a reanimate; in real life on his own world, he must have had an amazing potential for even that much to carry over. "We're dead. We're dead, and we're here, and they tell us to make helicopters. So we make them, working like dogs to make a deadline. Then, just as the first one comes off the line, the power fails. No more juice. The head engineer took off in the one we finished. He was going to find out what gives, but he never came back. So we sit." He spat on the ground. "I wish they'd left me dead after the plant blew up. I'm not myself since then."

"What in hell would they need with helicopters?" Hanson asked.

The man shrugged. "Beats me. But I'm beginning to figure some things out. They've got some kind of trouble with the sky. I figure they got confused in bringing us here. This shop is one that made those big cargo copters they call 'Sky Hooks' and maybe they thought the things were just what they're called. All I know is they kept us working five solid weeks for nothing. I knew the power was going to fail; they had the craziest damn generating plant you ever saw, and it couldn't last. The boilers kept sizzling and popping their safety valves with no fire in the box! Just some little old man sitting in a corner, practicing the Masonic grip or something over a smudgepot."

Hanson gestured back to the sheds. "If there's no power, what are those lights?"

"Witch lights, they told us," the man explained. "Saved a lot of wiring, or something. They — hey, what's that?"

He was looking up, and Hanson followed his gaze. There was something whizzing overhead at jet-plane speed. "A piece of the sky falling?" he said.

The man snorted. "Falling sidewise? Not likely, even here. I tell you, pal, I don't like this place. Nothing works right. There was no fuel for the 'copter we finished — the one we called Betsy Ann. But the little geezer who worked the smudgepot just walked up to it and wiggled his finger. 'Start your motor going, Betsy Ann,' he ordered with some other mumbo-jumbo. Then the motor roared and he and the engineer, took off at double the speed she could make on high-test gas. Hey, there it is again! Doesn't look like the Betsy Ann coming back, either."

The something whizzed by again, in the other direction, but lower and slower. It made a gigantic but erratic circle beyond the sheds and swooped back. It looked nothing like a helicopter. It looked like a Hallowe'en decoration of a woman on a broomstick. As it came nearer, Hanson saw that it *was* a woman on a broomstick, flying erratically. She straightened out in a flat glide.

She came in for a one-point landing a couple of yards away. The tip of the broom handle hit the ground, and she went sailing over it, to land on her hands and knees. She got up, facing the shed.

The woman was Nema. Her face was masklike, her eyes tortured. She was staring searchingly around her, looking at every man.

"Nema!" Hanson cried.

She spun to face him, and gasped. Her skin seemed to turn gray, and her eyes opened to double their normal size. She took one tottering step toward him and halted.

"Illusion!" she whispered hoarsely, and slumped to the ground in a faint.

She was reviving before he could raise her from the ground. She swayed a moment, staring at him. "You're not dead!"

"What's so wonderful about that around here?" he asked, but not with much interest. With the world going to pot and only a few days left, the girl's face and the slim young body under it were about all the reality left worth thinking about. He grabbed for her, pulling her to him. Bertha had never made him feel like that.

She managed to avoid his lips and slid away from him. "But they used the snetha-knife! Dave Hanson, you never died! It was only induced illusion by that — that Bork! And to think that I nearly died of grief while you were enjoying yourself here! You ... you mandrake-man!"

He grunted. He'd almost managed to forget what he was, and he didn't enjoy having the aircraft worker find out. He turned to see what the reaction was, and then stared open-mouthed at his surroundings.

There were no lights from the plane factory. In fact, there was no plane factory. In the half-light of the sky, he saw that the plant was gone. No men were left. There was only barren earth, with a tiny, limp sapling in the middle of empty acres.

"What happened?"

Nema glanced around briefly and sighed. "It's happening all over. They created the plane plant by the law of identities from that little plane tree sapling, I suppose; it is a plane plant, after all. But with the conjunctions and signs failing, all such creations are returning to their original form, unless a spell is used continually over them. Even then, sometimes, we fail. Most of the projects vanished after the sun fell."

Hanson remembered the man with whom he'd been talking before Nema appeared. He'd have liked to know such a man before death and revivification had ruined him. It wasn't fair that anyone with character enough to be that human even as a zombie should be wiped out without even a moment's consideration. Then he remembered the man's own estimate of his current situation. Maybe he was better off returned to the death that had claimed him.

Reluctantly, he returned to his own problems. "All right, then, if you thought I was dead, what are you doing here, Nema?"

"I felt the compulsion begin even before I returned to the city. I thought I was going mad. I tried to forget you, but the compulsion grew until I could fight it no longer." She shuddered. "It was a terrible flight. The carpets will not work at all now, and I could hardly control the broom. Sometimes it wouldn't lift. Twice it sailed so high I could hardly breathe. And I had no hope of finding you, yet I went on. I've been flying when I could for three days now."

Bork, of course, hadn't known of her spell with which she'd forced herself to want him "well and truly." Apparently it had gone on operating even when she thought he was dead, and with a built-in sense of his direction. Well, she was here — and he wasn't sorry.

Hanson took another look across the plains toward the glowing hell of the horizon. He reached for her and pulled her to him. She was firm and sweet against him, and she was trembling in response to his urging.

At the last moment she pulled back. "You forget yourself, Dave Hanson! I'm a registered and certified virgin. My blood is needed for — "

"For spells that won't work anyhow," he told her harshly. "The sky isn't falling now, kid. It's down — or most of it."

"But — " She hesitated and then let herself come a trifle closer. Her voice was doubtful. "It's true that our spells are failing. Not even the surest magic is reliable. The world has gone mad, and even magic is no longer trustworthy. But — "

He was just pulling her close enough again and feeling her arms lift to his neck when the ground shook behind them and there was a sound of great, jarring, thudding steps.

Hanson jerked around to see a great roc making its landing run, heading straight for them. The huge bird braked savagely, barely stopping before they were under its feet.

From its back, a ladder of some flexible material snaked down and men began descending. The first were mandrakes in the uniform of the Satheri, all carrying weapons with evil-looking blades or sharp stickers.

The last man off was Bork. He came toward Hanson and Nema with a broad grin on his face. "Greetings, Dave Hanson. You do manage to survive, don't you? And my little virgin sister, without whose flight I might not have found you. Well, come along. The roc's growing impatient!"

VIII

The great roc's hard-drumming wings set up a constant sound of rushing air and the distance flowed behind them. There was the rush of wind all around them, but on the bird's back they were in an area where everything seemed calm. Only when Hanson looked over toward the ground was he fully conscious of the speed they were making. From the height, he could see where the sun had landed. It was sinking slowly into the earth, lying in a great fused hole. For miles around, smaller drops of the three-mile-diameter sun had spattered and were etching deeper holes in the pitted landscape.

Then they began passing over desolate country, scoured by winds, gloomy from the angry, glaring clouds above. Once, two bodies went hurtling upwards toward the great gaps in the sky.

"Those risings were from men who were no worshippers of the egg's hatching," Bork commented. "It's spreading. Something is drawing them up from all over the planet."

Later, half a square mile of the shell cracked off. The roc squawked harshly, but it had learned and had been watching above. By a frantic effort of the great wings, it missed the hurtling chunk. They dropped a few thousand feet in the winds that followed the piece of sky, but their altitude was still safe.

Then they passed over a town, flying low. The sights below were out of a ghoul's bacchanalia. As the roc swept over, the people stopped their frenzied pursuit of sensation and ran for weapons. A cloud of arrows hissed upwards, all fortunately too late.

"They blame all their troubles on the magicians," Bork explained. "They've been shooting at everything that flies. Not a happy time to associate with the Satheri, is it?"

Nema drew further back from him. "We're not all cowards like you! Only rats desert a sinking ship."

"Nobody thought it was sinking when I deserted," Bork reminded her. "Anyhow, if you'd been using your eyes and seen the way we are traveling, you'd know I've rejoined the crew. I've made up with the Sather Karf — and at a time like this, our great grandfather was glad to have me back!"

Nema rushed toward him in delight, but Hanson wasn't convinced. "Why?" he asked.

Bork sobered. "One of the corpses that fell back from the risings added a word to what the others had said. No, I'll bear the weight of it myself, and not burden you with it. But I'm convinced now that his egg should not hatch. I had doubts before, unlike our friend Malok, who also heard the words but is doubly the fanatic now. Perhaps the hatching cannot be stopped — but I've decided that I am a man and must fight like one against the fates. So, though I still oppose much that the Satheri have done, I've gone back to them. We'll be at the camp of the Sather Karf shortly."

That sewed everything up neatly, Hanson thought. Before, he had been torn between two alternatives. Now there was only one and he had no choice; he could never trust the Sons of the Egg with Bork turned against them. He stared up at the sky, realizing that more than half of it had already fallen. The rest seemed too weak to last much longer. It probably didn't make much difference what he did now or who had him; time was running out for this world.

The light was dimmer by the time they reached the great capital city — or what was left of it. They had left the sun pyre far to the south. The air was growing cold already.

The roc flew low over the city. The few people on the streets looked up and made threatening gestures, but there was no flight of arrows from the ground. Probably the men below had lost even the strength to hate. It was hard to see, since there was no electric lighting system now. But it seemed to Hanson that only the oldest and ugliest buildings were still standing. Honest stone and metal could survive, but the work of magic was no longer safe.

One of the remaining buildings seemed to be a hospital, and the empty space in front of it was crammed with people. Most of them seemed to be dead or unconscious. Squat mandrakes were carrying off bodies toward a great fire that was burning in another square. Plague and pestilence had apparently gotten out of hand.

They flew on, beyond the city toward the construction camp that had been Hanson's head-quarters. The roc was beginning to drop into a long landing glide, and details below were easier to see. Along the beach beyond the city, a crowd had collected. They had a fire going and were preparing to cook one of the mermaids. A fight was already going on over the prey. Food must have been exhausted days before.

The camp was a mess when they reached it. One section had been ripped down by the lash of wind from a huge piece of the sky, which now lay among the ruins with a few stars glowing inside it. There was a brighter glow beyond. Apparently one blob of material from the sun had been tossed all the way here and had landed against a huge rock to spatter into fragments. The heat from those fragments cut through the chill in the air, and the glow furnished light for most of the camp.

The tents had been burned, but there was a new building where the main tent had been. This was obviously a hasty construction job, thrown together of rocks and tree trunks, without the use of magic. It was more of an enormous lean-to than a true building, but it was the best protection now available. Hanson could see Sather Karf and Sersa Garm waiting outside, together with less than a hundred other warlocks.

The mandrakes prodded Hanson down from the roc and toward the new building, then left at a wave of the Sather Karf's hand. The old man stared at Hanson intently, but his expression was unreadable. He seemed to have aged a thousand years. Finally he lifted his hand in faint greeting, sighed and dropped slowly to a seat. His face seemed to collapse, with the iron running out of it. He looked like a beaten, sick old man. His voice was toneless. "Fix the sky, Dave Hanson!"

There were angry murmurs from other warlocks in the background, but Sather Karf shook his head slowly, still facing Hanson. "No — what good to threaten dire punishments or to torture you when another day or week will see the end of everything? What good to demand your reasons for desertion when time is so short? Fix the sky and claim what reward you will afterwards. We have few powers now that the basis of astrology is ruined. But repair our sky and we can reward you beyond your dreams. We can find ways to return you to your own world intact. You have near immortality now. We can fill that entire lifetime with pleasures. We'll give you jewels to buy an empire. Or if it is vengeance against whatever you feel we are, you shall know my secret name and the name of everyone here. Do with us then what you like. *But fix the sky!*"

It shook Hanson. He had been prepared to face fury, or to try lying his way out if there was a chance with some story of having needed to study Menes's methods. Or of being lost. But he had no defense prepared against such an appeal.

It was utterly mad. He could do nothing, and their demands were impossible. But before the picture of the world dying and the decay of the old Sather's pride, even Hanson's own probable death with the dying world seemed unimportant. He might at least give them something to hope for while the end came.

"Maybe," he said slowly. "Maybe, if all of the men you brought here to work on the problem were to pool their knowledge, we might still find the answer. How long will it take to get them here for a council?"

Ser Perth appeared from the group. Hanson had thought the man dead in the ruins of the pyramid, but somehow he had survived. The fat was going from his face, and his mustache was untrimmed, but he was uninjured. He shook his head sadly. "Most have disappeared with their projects. Two escaped us. Menes is dead. Cagliostro tricked us successfully. You are all we have left. And we can't even supply labor beyond those you see here. The people no longer obey us, since we have no food to give them."

"You're the only hope," Bork agreed. "They've saved what they could of the tools from the camp and what magical instruments are still useful. They've held on only for your return."

Hanson stared at them and around at the collection of bric-a-brac and machinery they had assembled for him. He opened his mouth, and his laughter was a mockery of their hopes and of himself.

"Dave Hanson, world saver! You got the right name but the wrong man, Sather Karf," he said bitterly. He'd been a pretender long enough, and what punitive action they took now didn't seem to matter. "You wanted my uncle, David Arnold Hanson. But because his friends called him Dave and cut that name on his monument, and because I was christened by the name you called, you got me instead. He'd have been helpless here, probably, but with me you have no chance. I couldn't even build a doghouse. I wasn't even a construction engineer. Just a computer operator and repairman."

He regretted ruining their hopes, almost as he said it. But he could see no change on the old Sather's face. It seemed to stiffen slightly and become more thoughtful, but there was no disappointment.

"My grandson Bork told me all that," he said. "Yet your name was on the monument, and we drew you back by its use. Our ancient prophecy declared that we should find omnipotence carved on stone in a pool of water, as we found your name. Therefore, by the laws of rational magic, it is *you* to whom nothing is impossible. We may have mistaken the direction of your talent, but nonetheless it is you who must fix the sky. What form of wonder is a computer?"

Dave shook his head at the old man's monomania. "Just a tool. It's a little hard to explain, and it couldn't help."

"Humor my curiosity, then. What is a computer, Dave Hanson?"

Nema's hand rested on Hanson's arm pleadingly, and he shrugged. He groped about for some answer that could be phrased in their language, letting his mind flicker from the modern electronic gadgets back to the old-time tide predictor.

"An analogue computer is a machine that ... that sets up conditions mathematically similar to the conditions in some problem and then lets all the operations proceed while it draws a graph — a prediction — of how the real conditions would turn out. If the tides change with the position of some heavenly body, then we can build cams that have shapes like the effect of the moon's orbit, and gear them together in the right order. If there are many factors, we have a cam for each factor, shaped like the periodic rise and fall of that factor. They're all geared to let the various factors operate at the proper relative rate. With such a machine, we can run off a graph of the tides for years ahead. Oh, hell — it's a lot more complicated than that, but it takes the basic facts and draws a picture of the results. We use electronic ones now, but the results are the same."

"I understand," Sather Karf said. Dave doubted it, but he was happy to be saved from struggling with a more detailed explanation. And maybe the old man did understand some of it. He was no fool in his own subject, certainly. Sather Karf pondered for a moment, and then nodded with apparent satisfaction. "Your world was more advanced in understanding than I had thought. This computer is a fine scientific instrument, obeying natural law well. We have applied the same methods, though less elaborately. But the basic magical principle of similarity is the foundation of true science."

Dave started to protest, and then stopped, frowning. In a way, what the other had said was true. Maybe there was some relation between science and magic, after all; there might even be a meeting ground between the laws of the two worlds he knew. Computers set up similar conditions, with the idea that the results would apply to the original. Magic used some symbolic part of a thing in manipulations that were to be effective for the real thing. The essential difference was that science was predictive and magic was effective — though the end results were often the same. On Dave's world, the cardinal rule of logic was that the symbol was not the thing — and work done on symbols had to be translated by hard work into reality. Maybe things were really more logical here where the symbol was the thing, and all the steps in between thought and result were saved.

"So we are all at fault," Sather Karf said finally. "We should have studied you more deeply and you should have been more honest with us. Then we could have obtained a computer for you and you could have simulated our sky as it should be within your computer and forced it to be repaired long ago. But there's no time for regrets now. We cannot help you, so you must help yourself. Build a computer, Dave Hanson!"

"It's impossible."

Sudden rage burned on the old man's face, and he came to his feet. His arm jerked back and snapped forward. Nothing happened. He grimaced at the ruined sky. "Dave Hanson," he cried sharply, "by the unfailing power of your name which is all of you, I hold you in my mind and your throat is in my hand — "

The old hands squeezed suddenly, and Hanson felt a vise clamp down around his throat. He tried to break free, but there was no escape. The old man mumbled, and the vise was gone, but something clawed at Hanson's liver. Something else rasped across his sciatic nerve. His kidneys seemed to be wrenched out of him.

"You will build a computer," Sather Karf ordered. "And you *will* save our world!"

Hanson staggered from the shock of the pain, but he was no longer unused to agony. He had spent too many hours under the baking of the sun, the agony of the snetha-knife and the lash of an overseer's whip. The agony could not be stopped, but he'd learned it could be endured. His fantastic body could heal itself against whatever they did to him, and his mind refused to accept the torture supinely. He took a step toward Sather Karf, and another. His hands came up as he moved forward.

Bork laughed suddenly. "Let up, Sather Karf, or you'll regret it. By the laws, you're dealing with a *man* this time. Let up, or I'll free him to meet you fairly."

The old man's eyes blazed hotly. Then he sighed and relaxed. The clutching hands and the pain were gone from Hanson as the Sather Karf slumped back wearily to his seat.

"Fix our sky," the old man said woodenly.

Hanson staggered back, panting from his efforts. But he nodded. "All right," he agreed. "Like Bork, I think a man has to fight against his fate, no matter how little chance he has. I'll do what I can. I'll build the damned computer. But when I'm finished, I'll wait for *your* true name!"

Suddenly Sather Karf laughed. "Well said, Dave Hanson. You'll have my name when the time comes. And whatever else you desire. Also what poor help we can give you now. Ser Perth, bring food for Dave Hanson!"

Ser Perth shook his head sadly. "There is none. None at all. We hoped that the remaining planets would find a favorable conjunction, but — "

Dave Hanson studied his helpers with more bitterness. "Oh, hell!" he said at last. He snapped his fingers. "Abracadabra!"

His skill must be improving, since he got exactly what he had wished for. A full side of beef materialized against his palm, almost breaking his arm before he could snap it out of the way. The others swarmed hungrily toward it. At their expressions of wonder, Hanson felt more confidence returning to him. He concentrated and went through the little ritual again. This time loaves of bread rained down — fresh bread, and even of the brand he had wished for. Maybe he was becoming a magician himself, with a new magic that might still accomplish something.

Sather Karf smiled approvingly. "The theory of resonance, I see. Unreliable generally. More of an art than a science. But you show promise of remarkable natural ability to apply it."

"You know about it?" Dave had assumed that it was completely outside their experience and procedures.

"We *knew* it. But when more advanced techniques took over, most of us forgot it. The syllables resonate in a sound pattern with your world, to which you also still resonate. It won't work for you with anything from this world, nor will anything work thus for us from yours.

We had different syllables, of course, for use here." Sather Karf considered it. "But if you can control it and bring in one of your computers or the parts for one — "

Sixteen tries later, Dave was cursing as he stared at a pile of useless items. He'd gotten transistors at first. Then he lost control with too much tension or fatigue and began getting a bunch of assorted junk, such as old 201-A tubes, a transit, a crystal vase and resistors. But the chief trouble was that he couldn't secure working batteries. He had managed a few, but all were dead.

"Like the soul, electrical charges will not transfer," Sather Karf agreed sadly. "I should have told you that."

There was no electricity here with which to power anything, and their spells could not be made to work now. Even if he could build a computer out of what was obtainable, there would be no way to power it.

Overhead, the sky shattered with a roar, and another piece fell, tearing downwards toward the city. Sersa Garm stared upwards in horror.

"Mars!" he croaked. "Mars has fallen. Now can there be no conjunction ever!"

He tautened and his body rose slowly from the ground. A scream ripped from his lips and faded away as he began rushing upwards with increasing speed. He passed but of their sight, straight toward the new hole in the sky.

IX

In the hours that followed, Dave's vague plans changed a dozen times as he found each idea unworkable. His emotional balance was also erratic — though that was natural, since the stars were completely berserk in what was left of the sky. He seemed to fluctuate between bitter sureness of doom and a stupidly optimistic belief that something could be done to avert that doom. But whatever his mood, he went on working and scheming furiously. Maybe it was the desperate need to keep himself occupied that drove him, or perhaps it was the pleading he saw in the eyes around him. In the end, determination conquered his pessimism.

Somewhere in the combination of the science he had learned in his own world and the technique of magic that applied here there had to be an answer — or a means to hold back the end of the world until an answer could be found.

The biggest problem was the number of factors with which he had to deal. There were seven planets and the sun, and three thousand fixed stars. All had to be ordered in their courses, and the sky had to be complete in his calculations.

He had learned his trade where the answer was always to add one more circuit in increasing complexity. Now he had to think of the simplest possible similarity computer. Electronics was out, obviously. He tried to design a set of cams, like the tide machine, to make multiple tracings on paper similar to a continuous horoscope, but finally gave it up. They couldn't build the parts, even if there had been time.

He had to depend on what was available, since magic couldn't produce any needed device and since the people here had depended on magic too long to develop the other necessary skills. When only the broadest powers of magic remained, they were hopeless. Names were still potent, resonance worked within its limits, and the general principles of similarity still applied; but those were not enough for them. They depended too heavily on the second great principle of contagion, and that seemed to be wrapped up with some kind of association through the signs and houses and the courses of the planets.

He found himself thinking in circles of worry and pulled himself back to his problem. Normally, a computer was designed for flexibility and to handle varying conditions. This one could be designed to handle only one set of factors. It had to duplicate the courses of the objects in their sky and simulate the general behavior of the dome. It was not necessary to allow for all theoretical courses, but only for the normal orbits.

And finally he realized that he was thinking of a model — the one thing which is functionally the perfect analogue.

It brought him back to magic again. Make a doll like a man and stick pins in it — and the man dies. Make a model of the universe within the sky, and any changes in that should change reality. The symbol was the thing, and a model was obviously a symbol.

He began trying to plan a model with three thousand stars in their orbits, trying to find some simple way of moving them. The others watched in fascination. They apparently felt that the diagrams he was drawing were some kind of scientific spell. Ser Perth was closer than the others, studying the marks he made. The man suddenly pointed to his computations.

"Over and over I find the figure seven and the figure three thousand. I assume that the seven represents the planets. But what is the other figure?"

"The stars," Hanson told him impatiently.

Ser Perth shook his head. "That is wrong. There were only two thousand seven hundred and eighty-one before the beginnings of our trouble."

"And I suppose you've got the exact orbits of every one?" Hanson asked. He couldn't see that the difference was going to help much.

"Naturally. They are fixed stars, which means they move with the sky. Otherwise, why call them fixed stars? Only the sun and the planets move through the sky. The stars move with the sky over the world as a unity."

Dave grunted at his own stupidity. That really simplified things, since it meant only one control for all of them and the sky itself. But designing a machine to handle the planets and the sun, while a lot simpler, was still a complex problem. With time, it would have been easy enough, but there was no time for trial and error.

He ripped up his plans and began a new set. He'd need a glass sphere with dots on it for the stars, and some kind of levers to move the planets and sun. It would be something like the orreries he'd seen used for demonstrations of planetary movement.

Ser Perth came over again, staring down at the sketch. He drowned in doubt. "Why waste time drawing such engines? If you want a model to determine how the orbits should be, we have the finest orrery ever built here in the camp. We brought it with us when we moved, since it would be needed to determine how the sky should be repaired and to bring the time and the positions into congruence. Wait!"

He dashed off, calling two of the mandrakes after him. In a few minutes, they staggered back under a bulky affair in a protective plastic case. Ser Perth stripped off the case to reveal the orrery to Hanson.

It was a beautiful piece of workmanship. There was an enormous sphere of thin crystal to represent the sky. Precious gems showed the stars, affixed to the dome. The whole was nearly eight feet in diameter. Inside the crystal, Hanson could see a model of the world on jeweled-bearing supports. The planets and the sun were set on tracks around the outside, with a clockwork drive mechanism that moved them by means of stranded spiderweb cords. Power came from weights, like those used on an old-fashioned clock. It was obviously all hand work, which must make it a thing of tremendous value here.

"Sather Fareth spent his life designing this," Ser Perth said proudly. "It is so well designed that it can show the position of all things for a thousand centuries in the past or future by turning these cranks on the control, or it will hold the proper present positions for years from its own engine."

"It's beautiful workmanship," Hanson told him. "As good as the best done on my world."

Ser Perth went away, temporarily pleased with himself, and Hanson stood staring at the model. It was as good as he'd said it was — and completely damning to all of his theories and hopes. No model he could make would equal it. But in spite of it and all its precise analogy to the universe around him, the sky was still falling in shattered bits!

Sather Karf and Bork had come over to join Hanson. They waited expectantly, but Hanson could think of nothing to do. It had already been done — and had failed. The old man dropped a hand on his shoulder. There was the weight of all his centuries on the Sather, yet a curious toughness showed through his weariness. "What is wrong with the orrery?" he asked.

"Nothing — nothing at all, damn it!" Hanson told him. "You wanted a computer — and you've got it. You can feed in data as to the hour, day, month and year, turn the cranks, and the planets there will turn to their proper position exactly as the real planets should run. You don't need to read the results off graph paper. What more could any analogue computer do? But it doesn't influence the sky."

"It was never meant to," the old man said, surprise in his voice. "Such power — "

Then he stopped, staring at Hanson while something almost like awe spread over his face. "Yet ... the prophecy and the monument were right! You have unlocked the impossible! Yet you seem to know nothing of the laws of similarity or of magic, Dave Hanson. Is that crystal similar to the sky, by association, by contagion, or by true symbolism? A part may be a symbol for the whole — or so may any designated symbol, which may influence the thing it is. If I have a hair from your head, I can model you with power over you. But not with the hair of a pig! That is no true symbol!"

"Suppose we substituted bits of the real thing for these representations?" Hanson asked.

Bork nodded. "It might work. I've heard you found the sky material could be melted, and we've got enough of that where it struck the camp. Any one of us who has studied elementary alchemy could blow a globe of it to the right size for the sky dome. And there are a few stars from which we can chip pieces enough. We can polish them and put them into the sphere where they belong. And it will be risky, but we may even be able to shape a bit of the sun stuff to represent the great orb in the sky."

"What about the planets?" Hanson was beginning to feel the depression lift. "You might get a little of Mars, since it fell near here, but that still leaves the other six."

"That long associated with a thing achieves the nature of the thing," Sather Karf intoned, as if giving a lesson to a kindergarten student. "With the right colors, metals and bits of jewels — as well as more secret symbols — we can simulate the planets. Yet they cannot be suspended above the dome, as in this orrery — they must be within the sky, as in nature."

"How about putting some iron in each and using a magnet on the control tracks to move the planets?" Hanson suggested. "Or does cold iron ruin your conjuring here?"

Sather Karf snorted in obvious disgust, but Bork only grinned. "Why should it? You must have heard peasant superstitions. Still, you'd have a problem if two tracks met, as they do. The magnets would then affect both planets alike. Better make two identical planets for each — and two suns — and put one on your track controls. Then one must follow the other, though the one remain within the sky."

Hanson nodded. He'd have to shield the cord from the sun stuff, but that could be done. He wondered idly whether the real universe was going to wind up with tracks beyond the sky on which little duplicate planets ran — just how much similarity would there be between model and reality when this was done, if it worked at all? It probably didn't matter, and it could hardly be worse than whatever the risers had run into beyond the hole in the present sky. Metaphysics was a subject with which he wasn't yet fully prepared to cope.

The model of the world inside the orrery must have been made from earthly materials already, and it was colored to depict land and sea areas. It could probably be used. At their agreement, he nodded with some satisfaction. That should save some time, at least. He stared doubtfully at the rods and bearings that supported the model world in the center of the orrery.

"What about those things? How do we hold the globe in the center of everything?"

Bork shrugged. "It seems simple enough. We'll fashion supports of more of the sky material."

"And have real rods sticking up from the poles in the real universe?" Hanson asked sarcastically.

"Why not?" Bork seemed surprised at Hanson's tone. "There have always been such columns connecting the world and the sky. What else would keep us from falling?"

Hanson swore. He might have guessed it! The only wonder was that simple rods were used instead of elephants and turtles. And the doubly-damned fools had let Menes drive millions of slaves to death to build a pyramid to the sky when there were already natural columns that could have been used!

"There remains only one step," Sather Karf decided after a moment more. "To make symbol and thing congruent, all must be invoked with the true and secret name of the universe."

Hanson suddenly remembered legends of the tetragrammaton and the tales of magic he'd read in which there was always one element lacking. "And I suppose nobody knows that or dares to use it?"

There was hurt pride of the aged face and the ring of vast authority in his voice. "Then you suppose wrong, Dave Hanson! Since this world first came out of Duality, a Sather Karf has known that mystery! Make your device and I shall not fail in the invocation!"

For the first time, Hanson discovered that the warlocks could work when they had to, however much they disliked it. And at their own specialties, they were superb technicians. Under the orders of Sather Karf, the camp sprang into frenzied but orderly activity.

They lost a few mandrakes in prying loose some of the sun material, and more in getting a small sphere of it shaped. But the remainder gave them the heat to melt the sky stuff. When it came to glass blowing, Hanson had to admit they were experts; it should have come as no surprise, after the elaborate alchemical apparatus he'd seen. Once the crystal shell was cracked out of the orrery, a fat-faced Ser came in with a long tube and began working the molten sky material, getting the feel of it. He did things Hanson knew were nearly impossible, and he did them with the calm assurance of an expert. Even when another rift in the sky appeared with a crackling of thunder, there was no faltering on his part. The sky shell and world supports were blown into shape around the world model inside the outer tracks in one continuous operation. The Ser then clipped the stuff from his tube and sealed the tiny opening smoothly with a bit of sun material on the end of a long metal wand.

"Interesting material," he commented, as if only the technical nature of the stuff had offered any problem to him.

Tiny, carefully polished chips from the stars were ready, and men began placing them delicately on the shell. They sank into it at once and began twinkling. The planets had also been prepared, and they also went into the shell, while a mate to each was attached to the tracking mechanism. The tiny sun came last. Hanson fretted as he saw it sink into the shell, sure it would begin to melt the sky material. It seemed to have no effect, however; apparently the sun was not supposed to melt the sky when it was in place — so the little sun didn't melt the shell. Once he was sure of that, he used a scrap of the sky to insulate the second little sun that would control the first sympathetically from the track. He moved the control delicately by hand, and the little sun followed dutifully.

The weights on the control mechanism were in place, Hanson noted. Someone would probably have to keep them wound from now on, unless they could devise a foolproof motor. But that was for the future. He bent to the hand cranks. Sather Karf was being called to give the exact settings for this moment, but Hanson had a rough idea of where the planets should be. He began turning the crank, just as the Sather came up.

There was a slight movement. Then the crank stuck, and there was a whirring of slipping gears! The fools who had moved the orrery must have been so careless that they'd sprung the mechanism. He bent down to study the tiny little jeweled gears. A whole gear train was out of place!

Sather Karf was also inspecting it, and the words he cried didn't sound like an invocation, though they were strange enough. He straightened, still cursing. "Fix it!"

"I'll try," Hanson agreed doubtfully. "But you'd better get the man who made this. He'll know better than I — "

"He was killed in the first cracking of the sky when a piece hit him. Fix it, Dave Hanson. You claimed to be a repairman for such devices."

Hanson bent to study it again, using a diamond lens one of the warlocks handed him. It was a useful device, having about a hundred times magnification without the need for exact focusing. He stared at the jumble of fine gears, then glanced out through the open front: of the building toward the sky. There was even less of it showing than he had remembered. Most of the great dome was empty. And now there were suggestions of ...shadows ...in the empty spots. He looked away hastily, shaken.

"I'll need some fine tools," he said.

"They were lost in moving this," Ser Perth told him. "This is the best we can do."

The jumble of tools had obviously been salvaged from the kits on the tractors in the camp. There was one fairly small pair of pliers, a small pick and assorted useless junk. He shook his head hopelessly.

"Fix it!" Sather Karf ordered again. The old man's eyes were also on the sky. "You have ten minutes, perhaps — no more."

Hanson's fingers steadied as he found bits of wire and began improvising tools to manipulate the tiny gears. The mechanism was a piece of superb craftsmanship that should have lasted for a million years, but it had never been meant to withstand the heavy shock of being dropped, as it must have been. And there was very little space inside. It should have been disassembled and put back piece by piece, but there was no time for that.

Another thunder of falling sky sounded, and the ground heaved. "Earthquakes!" Sather Karf whispered. "The end is near!"

Then a shout went up, and Hanson jerked his eyes from the gears to focus on a group of rocs that were landing at the far end of the camp. Men were springing from their backs before they stopped running — men in dull robes with elaborate masks over their faces. At the front was Malok, leader of the Sons of the Egg, brandishing his knife.

His voice carried clearly. "The egg hatches! To the orrery and smash it! That was the shadow in the pool. Destroy it before Dave Hanson can complete his magic!"

The men behind him yelled. Around Hanson, the magicians cried out in shocked fear. Then old Sather Karf was dashing out from under the cover of the building, brandishing a pole on which a drop of the sun-stuff was glowing. His voice rose into a command that rang out over the cries of the others.

Dave reached for a heavy hammer, meaning to follow. The old Sather seemed to sense it without looking back. "Fix the engine, Dave Hanson," he called.

It made sense. The others could do the fighting, but only he had training with such mechanisms. He turned back to his work, just as the warlocks began rallying behind Sather Karf, grabbing up what weapons they could find. There was no magic in this fight. Sticks, stones, hammers and knives were all that remained workable.

Dave Hanson bent over the gears, cursing. Now there was another rumble of thunder from the falling sky. The half-light from the reflected sunlight dimmed, and the ground shook violently. Another set of gears broke from the housing. Hanson caught up a bit of sun-stuff on the sharp point of the awl and brought it closer, until it burned his hands. But he had seen enough. The mechanism was ruined beyond his chance to repair it in time.

He slapped the cover shut and stuck the sun-tipped awl where it would light as much of the orrery as possible. As always, the skills of his own world had failed. To the blazes with it, then — when in magic land, magic had to do.

He thought of calling Ser Perth or Sather Karf, but there was no time for that, and they could hardly have heard him over the sounds of the desperate fight going on.

He bent to the floor, searching until he found a ball of the sky material that had been pinched off when the little opening was sealed. Further hunting gave him a few bits of dust from the star bits and some of the junk that had gone into shaping the planets. He brushed in some dirt from the ground that had been touched by the sun stuff and was still glowing faintly. He wasn't at all sure of how much he could extrapolate from what he'd read in the book on Applied Semantics, but he knew he needed a control — a symbol of the symbol, in this case. It was crude, but it might serve to represent the orrery.

He clutched it in his hand and touched it against the orrery, trying to remember the formula for the giving of a true name. He had to improvise, but he got through a rough version of it, until he came to the end: "I who created you name you — " What the deuce did he name it? "I name you Rumpelstilsken and order you to obey me when I call you by your name."

He clutched the blob of material tighter in his hand, mentally trying to shape an order that wouldn't backfire, as such orders seemed to in the childhood stories of magic he had learned. Finally his lips whispered the simplest order he could find. "Rumpelstilsken, repair yourself!"

There was a whirring and scraping inside the mechanism, and Hanson let out a yell. He got only a hasty glimpse of gears that seemed to be back on their tracks before Sather Karf was beside him, driving the cranks with desperate speed.

"We have less than a minute!" the old voice gasped.

The Sather's fingers spun on the controls. Then he straightened, moving his hands toward the orrery in passes too rapid to be seen. There was a string of obvious ritual commands in their sacred language. Then a single word rang out, a string of sounds that should have come from no human vocal chords.

There was a wrench and twist through every atom of Hanson's body. The universe seemed to cry out. Over the horizon, a great burning disc rose and leaped toward the heavens as the sun went back to its place in the sky. The big bits of sky-stuff around also jerked upwards, revealing themselves by the wind they whipped up and by the holes they ripped through the roof of the building. Hanson clutched at the scrap he had pocketed, but it showed no sign of leaving, and the tiny blob of sun-stuff remained fixed to the awl.

Through the diamond lens, Hanson could see the model of the world in the orrery changing. There were clouds apparently painted on it where no clouds had been. And there was an indication of movement in the green of the forests and the blue of the oceans, as if trees were whipping in the wind and waves lapping the shores.

When he jerked his eyes upward, all seemed serene in the sky. Sunlight shone normally on the world, and from under the roof he could see the gaudy blue of sky, complete, with the cracks in it smoothing out as he watched.

The battle outside had stopped with the rising of the sun. Half the warlocks were lying motionless, and the other half had clustered together, close to the building where Hanson and Sather Karf stood. The Sons of the Egg seemed to have suffered less, since they greatly out-numbered the others, but they were obviously more shocked by the rising of the sun and the healing of the sky.

Then Malok's voice rang out sharply. "It isn't stable yet! Destroy the machine! The egg must hatch!"

He leaped forward, brandishing his knife, while the Sons of the Egg fell in behind him. The warlocks began to close ranks, falling back to make a stand under the jutting edge of the roof, where they could protect the orrery. Bork and Ser Perth were among them, bloody but hopelessly determined.

One look at Sather Karf's expression was enough to convince Hanson that Malok had cried the truth and that their work could still be undone. And it was obvious that the warlocks could never stand the charge of the Sons. Too many of them had already been killed, and there was no time for reviving them.

Sather Karf was starting forward into the battle, but Hanson made no move to follow. He snapped the diamond lens to his eye and his fingers caught at the drop of sun-stuff on the awl. He had to hold it near the glowing bit for steadiness, and it began searing his fingers. He forced control on his muscles and plunged his hand slowly through the sky sphere, easing the glowing blob downward toward the spot on the globe he had already located with the lens. His thumb and finger moved downward delicately, with all the skill of practice at working with nearly invisibly fine wires on delicate instruments.

Then he jerked his eyes away from the model and looked out. Something glaring and hot was suspended in the air five miles away. He moved his hand carefully, steadying it on one of the planet tracks. The glowing fire in the air outside moved another mile closer — then another. And now, around it, he could see a monstrous fingertip and something that might have been miles of thumbnail.

The warlocks leaped back under the roof. The Sons of the Egg screamed and panicked. Jerking horribly, the monstrous thing moved again. For part of a second, it hovered over the empty camp. Then it was gone.

Hanson began pulling his hand out through the shell of the model, whimpering as his other hand clenched against the blob in his pocket. He had suddenly realized what horrors were possible to anyone who could use the orrery now. "Rumpelstilsken, I command you to let no hand other than mine enter and to respond to no other controls." He hoped it would offer enough protection.

His hand came free and he threw the sun-bit away with a flick of his wrist. His hand ached with the impossible task of steadiness he had set it, and his finger and thumb burned and smoked. But the wound was already healing.

In the exposed section of the camp, the Sons of the Egg were charred corpses. There was a fire starting on the roof of the building, but others had already run out to quench that. It sounded like the snuffling progress of an undine across the roof! Maybe magic was working again.

Bork turned back from the sight of his former companions. His face was sick, but he managed to grin at Hanson. "Dave Hanson, to whom nothing is impossible," he said.

Hanson had located Nema finally as she approached. He caught her hand and grabbed Bork's arm. Like his own, it was trembling with fatigue and reaction.

"Come on," he said. "Let's find some place where we can see whether it's impossible now for you to magic up a decent meal. And a drink strong enough to scare away the sylphs."

The sylph that found them wasn't scared by the Scotch, but there was enough for all of them.

X

Three days can work magic — in a world where magic works. The planets swung along their paths again and the sun was in the most favorable house for conjuration. The universe was stable again.

There was food for all, and houses had been conjured hastily to shelter the people. The plagues were gone. Now the strange commerce and industry of this world were humming again. Those who had survived and those who could be revived were busily rebuilding. Some were missing, of course. Those who had risen and — hatched — were beyond recall, but no one spoke of them. If any Sons of the Egg survived, they were quiet in their defeat.

Hanson had been busy during most of the time. It had been taken for granted that he would tend to the orrery, setting it for the most favorable conditions when some special major work of magic required it, and he had taken the orders and moved the controls as they wanted them. The orrery was housed temporarily in the reconstituted hall of the Satheri in the capital city. They were building a new hall for it, to be constructed only of natural materials and hand labor, but that was a project that would take long months still.

Now the immediate pressure was gone, and Hanson was relaxing with Bork and Nema.

"Another week," Bork was saying. "Maybe less. And then gangs of the warlocks can spread out to fix up all the rest of the world — and to take over control of their slaves again. Are you happy with your victory, Dave Hanson?"

Hanson shrugged. He wasn't entirely sure, now. There was something in the looks of the Sather who gave him orders for new settings that bothered him. And some of the developments he watched were hardly what he would have preferred. The warlocks had good memories, it seemed, and there had been manifold offenses against them while the world was falling apart.

He tried to put it out of his mind as he drew Nema to him. She snuggled against him, admiring him with her eyes. But old habits were hard to break. "Don't, Dave. I'm a registered and certified — "

She stopped then, blushing, and Bork chuckled.

Ser Perth appeared at the doorway with two of the mandrakes. He motioned to Hanson. "The council of Satheri want you," he said. His eyes avoided the other, and he seemed uncomfortable.

"Why?" Bork asked.

"It's time for Dave Hanson's reward," Ser Perth said. The words were smooth enough, but the eyes turned away again.

Hanson got up and moved forward. He had been wondering when they would get around to this. Beside him, Bork and Nema also rose. "Never trust a Sather," Bork said softly.

Nema started to protest, then changed her mind. She frowned, torn between old and new loyalties.

"The summons was only for Dave Hanson," Ser Perth said sternly as the three drew up to him. But as Hanson took the arms of the other two, the Ser shrugged and fell in behind. Very softly, too low for the hearing of the mandrakes, his words sounded in Hanson's ear. "Guard yourself, Dave Hanson!"

So there was to be treachery, Hanson thought. He wasn't surprised. He was probably lucky to have even three friends. The Satheri would hardly feel very grateful to a mandrake-man who had accomplished something beyond their power, now that the crisis was over. They had always been a high-handed bunch, apparently, and he had served his purpose. But he covered his thoughts in a neutral expression and went forward quietly toward the huge council room.

The seventy leading Satheri were all present, with Sather Karf presiding, when Hanson was ushered into their presence. He moved down the aisle, not glancing at the seated Satheri, until he was facing the old man, drawing Nema and Bork with him. There were murmurs of protest, but nobody stopped him. Above him, the eyes of Sather Karf were uncertain. For a moment, there seemed to be a touch of friendliness and respect in them, but there was something else that Hanson liked far less. Any warmth that was there vanished at his first words.

"It's about time," Hanson said flatly. "When you wanted your world saved, you were free enough with offers of reward. But three days have passed without mention of it. Sather Karf, I demand your secret name!"

He heard Nema gasp, but felt Bork's fingers press against his arm reassuringly. There was a rising mutter of shock and anger from the others, but he lifted his voice over it. "And the secret names of all those present. That was also part of the promised reward."

"And do you think you could use the names, Dave Hanson?" Sather Karf asked. "Against the weight of all our knowledge, do you think you could become our master that easily?"

Hanson had his own doubts. There were counter-magical methods against nearly all magic, and the book he had read had been only an elementary one. But he nodded. "I think with your name I could get my hands on your hearts, even if you did your worst. It doesn't matter. I claim my reward."

"And you shall have it. The word of Sather Karf is good," the old man told him. "But there was no mention of when you would be given those names. You said that when the computer was finished you would *wait* for my true name, and I promised that you should have it when the time came, but not what the time would be. So you will wait, or the agreement shall be broken by you, not by me. When you are dying or otherwise beyond power over us, you shall have the names, Dave Hanson. No, hear me!"

He lifted his hand in a brief gesture and Hanson felt a thickness over his lips that made speech impossible.

"We have discussed your reward, and you shall indeed have it," Sather Karf went on. "Exactly as I promised it to you. I agreed to find ways to return you to your own world intact, and you shall be returned."

For a moment, the thickness seemed to relax, and Hanson choked a few words out through it. "What's the world of a mandrake-man, Sather Karf? A mandrake swamp?"

"For a mandrake-man, yes. But not for you." There was something like amusement in the old man's voice. "I never said you were a mandrake-man. That was told you by Ser Perth who knew no better. No, Dave Hanson, you were too important to us for that. Mandrake-men are always less than true men, and we needed your best. You were conjured atom by atom, id and ka and soul, from your world. Even the soul may be brought over when enough masters of magic work together and you were our greatest conjuration. Even then, we almost failed. But you're no mandrake-man."

A load of sickness seemed to leave Hanson's mind. He had never fully realized how much the shame of what he thought himself to be had weighed on him. Then his mind adjusted to the new facts, dismissing his past worries.

"I promised you that we would fill your entire lifetime with pleasures," Sather Karf went on. "And you were assured of jewels to buy an empire. All this the council is prepared to give you. Are you ready for your reward?"

"No!" Bork's cry broke out before Hanson could answer. The big man was writhing before he could finish the word, but his own fingers were working in conjurations that seemed to hold back enough of the spells against him to let him speak. "Dave Hanson, your world was a world of rigid laws. You died there. And there would be no magic to avoid the fact that there you must always be dead."

Hanson's eyes riveted on the face of Sather Karf. The old man looked back and finally nodded his head. "That is true," he admitted. "It would have been kinder for you not to know, but it is the truth."

"And jewels enough to buy an empire on a corpse," Hanson accused. "A lifetime of pleasures — simple enough when that lifetime would be over before it began. What were the pleasures, Sather Karf? Having you reveal your name just before I was sent back and feeling I'd won?" He grimaced. "I reject the empty rewards of your empty promises!"

"I also rejected the interpretation, but I was out-voted," Sather Karf said, and there was a curious reluctance as he raised his hand. "But it is too late. Dave Hanson prepare to receive your reward. By the power of your name — "

Hanson's hand went to his pocket and squeezed down on the blob of sky material there. He opened his mouth, and found that the thickness was back. For a split second, his mind screamed in panic as he realized he could not even pronounce the needed words.

Then coldness settled over his thoughts as he drove them to shape the unvoiced words in his mind. Nobody had told him that magic incantations had to be pronounced aloud. It seemed to be the general law, but for all he knew, ignorance of the law here might change the law. At least he meant to die trying, if he failed.

"Rumpelstilsken, I command the sun to set!"

He seemed to sense a hesitation in his mind, and then the impression of jeweled gears turning. Outside the window, the light reddened, dimmed, and was gone, leaving the big room illuminated by only a few witch lights.

The words Sather Karf had been intoning came to a sudden stop, even before they could be drowned in the shouts of shock and panic from the others. His eyes centered questioningly on Hanson and the flicker of a smile crossed his face. "To the orrery!" he ordered. "Use the manual controls."

Hanson waited until he estimated the men who left would be at the controls. The he clutched the sky-blob again. The thoughts in his mind were clearer this time.

"Rumpelstilsken, let the sun rise from the west and set in the east!"

Some of the Satheri were at the windows to watch what happened this time. Their shouts were more frightened than before. A minute later, the others were back, screaming out the news that the manual controls could not be moved — could not even be touched.

The orrery named Rumpelstilsken was obeying its orders fully, and the universe was obeying its symbol.

Somehow, old Sather Karf brought order out of the frightened mob that had been the greatest Satheri in the world. "All right, Dave Hanson," he said calmly. "Return the sun to its course. We agree to your conditions."

"You haven't heard them yet!"

"Nevertheless," Sather Karf answered firmly, "we agree. What else can we do? If you decided to wreck the sky again, even you might not be able to repair it a second time." He tapped his hands lightly together and the sound of a huge gong reverberated in the room. "Let the hall be cleared. I will accept the conditions in private."

There were no objections. A minute later Hanson, Bork and Nema were alone with the old man. Sunlight streamed in through the window, and there were fleecy clouds showing in the blue sky.

"Well?" Sather Karf asked. There was a trace of a smile on his face and a glow of what seemed to be amusement in his eyes as he listened, though Hanson could see nothing amusing in the suggestions he was making.

First, of course, he meant to stay here. There was no other place for him, but he would have chosen to stay in any event. Here he had developed into what he had never even thought of being, and there were still things to be learned. He'd gone a long way on what he'd found in one elementary book. Now, with a chance to study all their magical lore and apply it with the methods he had learned in his own world, there were amazing possibilities opening up to him. For the world, a few changes would be needed. Magic should be limited to what magic did best; the people needed to grow their own food and care for themselves. And they needed protection from the magicians. There would have to be a code of ethics to be worked out later.

"You've got all the time you need to work things out, Sathator Hanson," Sather Karf told him. "It's your world, literally, so take your time. What do you want first?"

Hanson considered it, while Nema's hand crept into his. Then he grinned. "I guess I want to get your great granddaughter turned into a registered and certified wife and take her on a long honeymoon," he decided. "After what you've put me through, I need a rest."

He took her arm and started down the aisle of the council room. Behind him, he heard Bork's chuckle and the soft laughter of Sather Karf. But their faces were sobering by the time he reached the doorway and looked back.

"I like him, too, grandfather," Bork was saying. "Well, it seems your group was right, after all. Your prophecy is fulfilled. He may have a little trouble with so many knowing his name, but he's Dave Hanson, to whom nothing is impossible. You should have considered all the implications of omnipotence."

Sather Karf nodded. "Perhaps. And perhaps your group was also right, Bork. It seems that the world-egg has hatched." His eyes lifted and centered on the doorway.

Hanson puzzled over their words briefly as he closed the door and went out with Nema. He'd probably have to do something about his name, but the rest of the conversation was a mystery to him. Then he dismissed it. He could always remember it when he had more time to think about it.

It was many millenia and several universes later when Dave Hanson finally remembered. By then it was no mystery, of course. And there was no one who dared pronounce his true name.

THE END.